SECOND CHOICE

CUBS FOR RENT #8

CHARITY PARKERSON

--Warning: This book is intended for readers over the age of 18.

Created with Vellum

INTRODUCTION

Neither Clint nor Lynx can have who they want. It only seems natural to pass their time together. Until their second choice starts to feel a lot like their first, that is.

Clint has spent his life hiding his sexuality to the point of destroying everything. He didn't change until his secrets cost him the love of his life. Now he's determined to be different, even though it's too late. He has to change for himself. That turns out to be easier than he likes, since his new best friend is as eccentric and out as they come.

Since Lynx was five, he's been in love with the same guy. Unfortunately, that guy was too blind to see it and Lynx was too scared to lose a friend to push. Now he's lost his shot and trying to move on. Clint seems like just the distraction he needs. Until that diversion becomes an obsession, and now Lynx doesn't know what to do.

Two men who think they've lost their chance are about to learn that sometimes love is better the second time around. If only they can stop themselves from self-destructing... again.

ONE

SOMETIMES... WELL, MOST TIMES, CLINT WAS HIS own worst enemy. He would try to stick to the path he wanted to be on, but his thoughts always undermined him. That was why he had gone to Howling Twister tonight. The backwoods honkytonk had been his drinking hole many times in the past. This was his first visit since the rumors had started to spread about his sexuality. The moment Clint stepped through the door, he felt the difference in the air. People openly stared or lowered their eyes. Men Clint had known for years turned away—like they hoped Clint wouldn't recognize them. It might have been a blow, if he thought enough about any of them to care.

Loud music beat against Clint's ears as he leaned

against the bar. The cold beer in his hand didn't soothe the growing raw spot in his throat. It had nothing to do with no one speaking to him. He didn't know how to be the person he was. Clint couldn't change the way he was born, but goddamn. He didn't want to feel this way. While he had never felt like he fit in anywhere before his secrets became public knowledge, he had at least been able to fake it and go wherever he liked. Just when he thought the pressure in his chest would suffocate him, Clint's phone buzzed in his back pocket. He set his beer aside and dug out the device. A smile pulled at the corners of his mouth as he spotted Lynx's name. Lynx Hirata looked as crazy as his name. Bright and multi-colored Mohawk. His Asian descent gave him a sexy summertime glow year round. Skinny, short, and with green eyes that saw all the way to Clint's soul, Lynx kept Clint sane. He had jumped into Cint's life with both feet after a single meeting. Clint would go as far as to say that Lynx was his best friend. Of course, Hudson might fight him for that title. Clint clicked the message, opening it.

Lynx: *With Cage and Hudson married now, I don't think I should go over there and bug them quite so often, but I'm bored as shit. What are you doing tonight?*

Clint: *I was just wondering what you're doing tonight.*

Clint stared at his phone, smiling like an idiot while waiting for Lynx's response. It was ridiculous how happy just the thought of Lynx made him. The guy never stopped talking and he said the weirdest shit, but he made the world seem a little brighter.

"Did you hear from one of your little gay pals?"

Clint's chin shot up at the question. Jake Drowley stood smirking at his side. Clint had always hated Jake's slimy smile and greasy hair. He just looked like a guy who would say some asshole shit like that. Considering he was five-five and likely only one-sixty soaking wet, he shouldn't be looking so cocky. "Jake." It was all the greeting Clint could muster and his dislike still dripped from the single-word greeting. Clint outweighed the guy by nearly a hundred pounds and stood an inch shy of a foot taller.

Jake didn't seem to notice his disadvantaged size or was too drunk to be scared. "You didn't answer my question. The way you were smiling, I'd say you're making plans to go poop pounding tonight."

His phone buzzed. The strangest thought hit in the middle of his rising temper. It brought a smile to his face. Clint wondered how Lynx would handle this. He took a step closer to Jake, letting his smile grow as he stared down at the guy. "I wasn't, but now you're here." The sultry hint to Clint's voice left no doubt what he meant. "I mean, you noticed my smile. Not many men pay attention to things like that."

Jake walked away.

"What? I can't even get your number?" Clint yelled at his back. A chuckle rose in Clint's throat as Jake picked up the pace, scurrying away. With a shake of his head, Clint went back to reading Lynx's text. He missed him.

Lynx: *Would you like to go do something or come over? It's unnatural for us to be doing nothing on a Saturday night when we're single.*

Without a single thought, Clint's feet were already headed for the door. His mind had been made up without having to think about it. Clint shouldn't have come here in the first place. Lynx would teach him a better way. After all, Lynx had already saved him from one fight and trip to jail tonight without even realizing it. Clint wanted to know what else he had to offer.

Clint: *I'm on my way.*

THE CARPET PROBABLY LOOKED THREADBARE where Lynx had been pacing all night. Some days, Lynx had more to do than he had hours in the day. On those days, Lynx didn't think about Cage being married now. Even though he had given up hope a long time ago that Cage would ever notice him, and Lynx had his sights set on someone different now, he still had a raw spot in his heart where his secret love for Cage used to be. He had fallen in love with his best friend Cage when they met on the first day of school at five. Of course, those feelings hadn't turned into a romantic love until years later, but Cage had never looked at Lynx with the same level of affection. Not even after the first time they kissed or when things had gone further. Cage had still only seen Lynx as a friend. Lynx had never been willing to wreck their friendship to try for more.

For many years, Lynx had been all Cage had. After an attack left Cage badly scarred, he had retreated from the world. If Lynx had taken a chance on love, maybe Cage would have let him, if only so he wouldn't lose his only lifeline to the outside world. Lynx couldn't live with that. He couldn't spend the rest of his life wondering if Cage loved him only out of desperation, so he wouldn't be alone. So Lynx had stuck around, watching and waiting.

Quietly hoping. His patience had been for nothing. Cage had hired an assistant and fallen in love with him. Now they were happily married, and Lynx was the outsider. It was fine. Lynx loved Cage enough to want him to be happy, even if that happiness did not include him.

Plus, without Cage falling for that assistant, Lynx never would have met Clint. Lynx took a breath. Butterflies stirred in his gut. Clint was massive—like a bull. He was six feet and six inches of lickable cowboy. Clint's strawberry blond hair was a tad long in the back, curling at the ends. A slightly darker shade of red hair covered his jaw. His entire demeanor screamed hardened rancher. While he rarely smiled, he watched Lynx with a heat that kept Lynx's blood stirring. Honest to God, Lynx had never been more turned on by anyone, not even Cage. Lynx really wanted to taste him.

The doorbell buzzed, pulling Lynx from the fantasy of being in Clint's bed. Lynx cast a quick glance at the security camera before heading for the door. He released a loud, cat-like *rawrr* when he found Clint's large frame filling the entire doorway.

Clint snorted at the sound. "What was that?"

"That was me picturing all the things I could do with your gorgeous body."

At his claim, Clint shook his head. He never took Lynx seriously. That was why Lynx never hesitated to give Clint his every thought. As always, Clint pretended Lynx hadn't been flirting. "Let's go do something. I don't want to stay in tonight."

Clint looked restless. His eyes sparkled with need—like he had been trapped inside the house too long. Lynx's mind raced through a list of local events and bars. A smile tugged at his lips. It felt evil. Lynx waved him inside. "Come on. While I'm thinking I should make you go to your first gay bar, because you really need that experience under your belt, I have a different idea instead. I just need to grab a few things, and we'll go." He motioned for Clint to stay put as he closed the door behind him. "I'll be right back." Lynx rushed to his office. He hurriedly threw some things in a duffle bag and rushed back out to Clint. If they sped and blew through some red lights, they might have just enough time to enjoy two hours of play before the event closed for the night "Come on. I'll drive," he offered as he headed through the kitchen and toward the garage with Clint on his heels.

Thankfully, Clint didn't question him. Lynx didn't think he would willingly agree to Lynx's plans, so Lynx didn't intend to give him a chance to balk.

Clint followed like he trusted Lynx completely. That was good. Lynx was about to test the strength of that certainty.

Clint made it all of twenty minutes, holding on for dear life to the oh-shit handle, while Lynx zipped through town in his twenty-year-old Honda. "Um. Are we late?"

"A little." Lynx jumped onto the interstate for one exit and sped off again, flitting through traffic like he was playing a high-speed video game. They were cutting things close, but Lynx always drove like this. His car was like an old friend. They worked well together. Clint looked like he had been squashed into a can of Spam with his huge frame filling the passenger seat. Even though he looked slightly terrified, Clint didn't complain. It was possible he was too scared of distracting Lynx. The thought had Lynx fighting back a smile.

Lynx spotted the parking garage he had been searching for and stood on the brakes. For a moment, it felt like the tires left the ground as Lynx turned hard to the right, skidding between the two concrete barriers before stopping inches from the bright yellow bar that blocked the garage. He tapped his thumb on the steering wheel in his impatience as he waited for the machine to spit out his ticket and set him free. The moment the bar was high enough for Lynx to zip beneath, he was off again. He didn't bother looking for a spot on the bottom floors. They were too late for that. Instead, he took the corners at three times the set speed limit until he hit the top floor. Lynx slid into the first open spot. He checked his watch.

"Cool. Exactly two hours to play." He popped the trunk and jumped from the car. Clint followed at a slower pace. He looked a little pale. Lynx pointed at the ground beside him as he lifted the trunk's lid. "Stand right here. I'll help you dress."

"Help me dress?" Clint asked even as he moved to obey.

Lynx nodded absently and pulled out a set of robes. "You're a lot bigger than me, but wizarding robes are pretty forgiving." He paused as a thought hit. "I bet they have a vendor here selling these. I should buy you a set." He waved off his own thoughts. "You can wear these, and I'll buy you a set for next time." His gaze finally landed on Clint.

Clint looked horrified. "What do you mean?"

There was no mercy in Lynx's heart. Clint needed to learn the meaning of fun. "Leave your cowboy hat in the trunk. It doesn't go with this."

Clint's normal hard expression seemed twice as

harsh in the garage's bad lighting. He didn't take off his hat. "What are we doing?"

With a sigh, Lynx swept Clint's hat from his head. He bit back another cat-like growl. Damn. He just wanted to climb Clint like a sexy tree and hump him. Instead, Lynx tossed the hat in the trunk.

He slung one of the black robes from his duffle bag across Clint's shoulders. It was way too short. He tried to not let that bother him too much. There was nothing he could do about it until he found a vendor. "We're going to a wizard convention. They have vendors selling things and whatnot. It's fun. You'll see. Hold this," he said, passing Clint a wand. He dug out some fake glasses next and set them on Clint's face. They didn't hurt his hotness level in the least. In fact, Lynx had to tear his gaze away to find his own costume. By the time he popped his pair of glasses on, Clint had been holding the wand out like a snake long enough for it to be funny.

A chuckle escaped Lynx. "Don't look like that. Everyone will be dressed the same. We'll blend right in." Well, Lynx would. Clint was too tall and broad-shouldered to blend. Still, he didn't want Clint to freak out and refuse to go.

Lynx forced Clint's arm down and straightened his robes. "Now, we might get some weird looks on the way into the convention center, but fuck those people. They have no idea what they're missing by being sticks in the mud. If you start feeling too embarrassed along the way, just do what I always do —be even more outrageous so they go home with a story to tell." Lynx smirked. "Those people have no idea how much they need people like us. Otherwise, they wouldn't have anything to talk about." Lynx stuffed a wand in his front pocket and closed his trunk. "Ready?"

"I suppose."

At least he was game, even if he didn't look happy about it. Before they made it to the elevator, they encountered a group of drunk college-age students who were obviously parked there only to hop bars along the downtown stretch.

Two of the boys whistled. "Nerd alert."

"I'm uncomfortable," Clint muttered under his breath.

Lynx stepped closer to Clint until their brushing robes hid their hands. He took Clint's hand and squeezed. Lynx lowered his voice for Clint's ears alone. "Just think WWLD, what would Lynx do, and you'll be fine."

Clint's step slowed. "Okay." In a flash, the world spun as he found himself swept into Clint's arms.

The air left Lynx's lungs as Clint squeezed him to his massive chest. Clint's mouth covered his. Lynx's every muscle seized and then melted. His arms encircled Clint's neck. His fingers immediately found Clint's hair. Lynx's body responded like a lust spell had been cast over him. The world disappeared. If the rowdy group of drunkards were still watching, Lynx wouldn't know. He lost track of everything but Clint's tongue roughly stroking his. Lynx felt like he was being consumed. Clint squeezed Lynx's ass as he ground the lower half of their bodies together. Lynx had never been closer to coming in his jeans. Lynx's feet touched back down on the ground. Clint's kiss softened as his lips moved from Lynx's mouth to his jaw and on to his ear.

Each ragged breath Clint blew across Lynx's ear made goosebumps rise on Lynx's skin. "I'd see if I could get you off in your jeans if that wand wasn't stabbing me. Let's go check out this convention."

Clint stepped away and headed for the elevator like nothing happened. Lynx had to force his legs to move. They felt like lifeless weights he had to drag along for every step. A slight haze coated his vision with all the blood south of his brain. Lynx didn't know how to act, but he knew one thing with absolute certainty. One day soon, he would rock Clint's world. It was inevitable.

———

EVERY TIME CLINT FOUND HIMSELF OUT OF HIS comfort zone, he always gave himself the same internal speech: he had wanted to change and that was certainly happening. Years ago, when Clint met his ex, Colt, he had been determined no one would ever know. Clint had done horrible things to keep Colt a secret. To his mind, there was no scenario where he could allow a single soul see them as much as kiss. It was one thing to crave the touch of another man. It was a whole other to let anyone know that he did. That path had led to Clint losing the only person he ever loved.

So Clint would change. He had been fighting the urge to kiss Lynx for a while now. When those drunk kids had taunted them, something inside Clint burst free. He saw his moment to be free. To be different. He had seized his chance. Clint bit back a smile. He had no regrets. Fuck him. Lynx kissed like a man who had been waiting for it. The sounds he made had Clint hard as steel. Lynx hadn't held back. Clint could already picture Lynx tearing at his skin. He wouldn't be anyone's passive lover. Clint didn't want to wait, but he would, because Clint had sworn he would change, and Lynx wanted to do this wizard thing. So they would.

Lynx was right about them fitting in the moment they stepped inside. They were nowhere near as heavily costumed as some people. While Lynx had obviously thrown something together for them, other people looked as if they had invested hundreds of dollars into perfecting their look. People fought in invisible duels and posed for pictures. To Clint's surprise, Lynx was immediately overrun by people wanting autographs and their picture taken beside him. Clint smiled while watching Lynx in his element. In a way, he had known Lynx was successful in his field. He just hadn't realized Lynx was famous among a certain set.

"Are you Lynx's bodyguard?"

It took Clint a moment to realize the question was directed toward him. He blinked at the brown-haired girl like an idiot while considering his answer. Obviously, he wasn't Lynx's paid security, but he also didn't know how to respond. Clint would protect Lynx with his life, though.

"In a matter of speaking," he finally said, sounding uncertain even to his ears.

She shoved a phone into his hands, smiling brightly. "Would you take our picture?"

Once Clint took one photo, it was over. Phones flew his way from every direction. It seemed like he took a hundred or more photos before the crowd finally dispersed.

Lynx glanced at his watch. "Damn. We need to hurry." After grabbing Clint's hand, Lynx was off, and dragging him from one aisle to the next. Lynx oohed and aahed at everything he passed until he pulled Clint to a stop at a corner booth where robes were sold. He dug through the piles, talking a mile a minute about different colors matching different personalities and some other such shit Clint didn't understand. All Clint could do was stand still and let the tornado known as Lynx blow around him.

In a matter of moments, Clint stood in a black robe that covered him completely. Lynx's bright smile kept Clint from balking. "That's perfect. Now you'll be set to come back tomorrow."

"What?"

Lynx turned away and paid for the costume—like Clint hadn't spoken.

Clint didn't give up. "Did you say we're coming back tomorrow?"

Lynx continued to ignore him until he held a

huge bag of new costumes. He handed it to Clint. "They close in ten minutes, and we didn't get to do anything tonight. Plus, I bought Hudson and Cage robes too. Don't you want to see me force Hudson into this?" A loud bark of happy-sounding laughter escaped Lynx. "He'll die."

That happy laugh was the last thing Clint heard. If Lynx was smiling, then they would be back tomorrow. It was addicting being around someone who seemed genuinely happy. Lynx was like standing in the sunshine while adrenaline pumped through his veins. Clint didn't want it to stop. He didn't want to give up any time with Lynx. That didn't mean they would always be doing whatever crazy thing Lynx had planned.

"Since I did your thing and have to again tomorrow, is it my turn to pick what we do now?"

Lynx shrugged. "Sure. What do you have in mind?"

Clint shook his head. "Nope. You got to keep your plans a secret. I get the same. Let's drop your car off at your place." Lynx didn't argue, but then again, Lynx never argued. He was always happy to do whatever Clint suggested. He simply headed out with Clint trailing behind him just enough to stare at Lynx without guilt. Lynx was skinny but nicely shaped. Not that anyone could tell in his wizard robes. That kiss was fucking with Clint. Of course, it didn't help that he hadn't had sex in ages. He couldn't lie to himself, though. Wanting Lynx had nothing to do with being deprived. Lynx was so full of life and energy. He practically sparkled. His eyes were gorgeous and always twinkling with happiness. Maybe Clint's heart was a mess, but his body was completely on board with being with Lynx, and he didn't think Lynx had any qualms about being with him either.

Lynx's driving soon set Clint free from his crippling lust. Between the heavy metal music blasting against his eardrums and Lynx taking every corner at twice the speed limit, all Clint could do was hang on and pray they didn't die. Lynx did everything at top speed. Drive. Walk. Talk. He was a hurricane. When they swapped cars and Clint took over with a normal-person radio volume and a speed that would ensure they arrived unharmed, everything felt wrong—like life moved too slow.

"You can control the radio if you want." Even Clint blinked in surprise as the words left his lips. Sometimes, he had a bad feeling Lynx was rubbing off on him.

Lynx chuckled like a kid who had been given the

key to the sugar pantry. Instead of blasting out tunes, Lynx turned the radio off. "If I'm in control, I have questions."

Clint's cheeks ached, making him realize how hard he was smiling. Clint rarely smiled and meant it. Lynx brought out the best in him. That was one of the many reasons Clint couldn't stay away. "All right." After all, he wanted to know everything about Lynx too. For all Lynx's nonstop talking, he rarely talked about himself.

"Why don't you ever talk about your family?"

Like that, Clint's smile disappeared. "Jumping in with both feet, huh?"

Lynx huffed. It was adorable. "How is asking about your family jumping in with both feet? That's a harmless get-to-know-you-better question."

Clint cast a quick disbelieving look Lynx's way. "Is it harmless? Because I've got to say, you never talk about your family either."

From the corner of his eye, Clint saw Lynx wave his arms wildly. "That's unfair. My family is complete shit. Well, my mom is okay, but she's the only one."

"Mhmm," Clint hummed noncommittally. "Well," he shifted in his seat, leaning his elbow on the console in the center and finding a more comfortable spot before delving into an uncomfortable topic. "My dad was very much the typical good ol' boy. He worked hard and expected his wife and son to work just as hard at their designated roles. I guess those expectations chafed equally for Mom as they did me. She fell in love with a ranch hand and left everything behind when I was twenty-five. I suppose she thought she had done her duty by me and it was her turn to live. Dad—who had never shown an ounce of love to either of us—went out to the barn and hung himself the day after their divorce was finalized. That way, he never had to pay a single day of alimony and I got everything. Truth be told, and at the expense of sounding heartless, it was the nicest thing he ever did for me. Mom never came around again."

"Well, damn. I really was jumping in with both feet."

A chuckle sneaked out without permission. "It's fine. You can ask me anything you want. I don't have any secrets."

"Okay." Lynx wasn't one to be held back. "Can I try on your hat?"

The smile was back. Clint tilted his head Lynx's way. "Go for it."

With childlike glee, Lynx plucked the hat from Clint's head and plopped it on.

Clint couldn't stop his gaze from sliding Lynx's way for a quick peek. The hat fell to Lynx's ears—like a kid wearing his dad's hat. Clint's smile grew. "Very sexy."

Lynx dropped the sun visor and looked in the mirror. "Do you think so? I've never been much of a hat wearer. My hair is too awesome to hide, but I always suspected I could rock a cowboy hat."

"I imagine you could pull off any look you want with flair." Clint steered down his driveway, circling his lakeside cabin and parking near the back door. He killed the engine.

Lynx looked around. "I've been so focused on you and this hat, I haven't paid much attention to where we were going. Your plans for us are at your house? Kinky."

"Not exactly," Clint said cryptically as he slid from the truck. "Come help me decide what to pack to drink in the ice chest."

Lynx obediently followed him inside the house still wearing Clint's hat. Clint let him keep it. Lynx finally took it off and set it on the kitchen counter. After they spent a few minutes dumping ice in a small chest over what was left of a case of beer, they headed back out. Clint carried the cooler and led the way down to the dock. He didn't check Lynx's reaction as he nodded toward his boat. "Climb aboard."

To his surprise, Lynx deftly scrambled onto the small yacht, bobbing on the lake—like he had done it a thousand times. Of course, Clint recognized Lynx probably had. Clint followed right behind him.

Clint kept going until he had Lynx herded onto the sun deck. He set the cooler aside and settled down onto his ass. Lynx sat too. Clint popped open the cooler and passed a beer to Lynx before grabbing one for himself. Lynx was unusually quiet as they settled in to stargaze.

Clint couldn't take the silence. "I sit out here a lot at night. When I bought the boat, I planned to spend a lot of time on the water. Instead, I ended up doing this."

"This is awesome. It's quiet."

Clint chuckled at Lynx's assessment. "I wouldn't have thought you care much for silence."

"Just because I'm never quiet doesn't mean I don't like the silence." Lynx sounded slightly offended. As if determined to prove Clint wrong, Lynx drank his beer and stared at the night sky. He lasted all of thirty seconds. "Do you believe in aliens?"

Clint didn't laugh. He was used to Lynx's randomness. He glanced at the sky and thought over the question before answering. "I don't know. Since I've never seen one, I can't say one way or the other." Clint wasn't a dreamer like Lynx. He was more of a realist.

"I believe," Lynx said before Clint could ask in kind. "The universe is just so big. I mean, it's endless," he said, sweeping an arm toward the sky. "It seems the height of arrogance to believe we're the only lifeforms floating around in its vastness."

Clint loved the way Lynx's mind worked. He was always on the move—like he couldn't sit still, or his mind was too full for him to stop. Clint wanted more. He needed Lynx's thoughts

"Do you have a theory on why our planet isn't crawling with a countless variety of alien life? I mean, Earth is old. Shouldn't we be a huge mixture of alien races by now?"

Lynx chuckled as if Clint had no idea what he was in for with that line of questioning. Little did he know, Clint couldn't wait for the floodgates of nerdom to open and drown him. Lynx didn't disappoint.

"Well, first off, who's to say the planet isn't already crawling with alien life? But would you come here if you had any other choice? I mean, we pollute our air and water nonstop, killing off beautiful wildlife in the process. There's always a war somewhere and people hate other people based on made-up beliefs while teaching every new generation their intolerance. Aliens probably lock their doors when they fly past us."

A smile burst from Clint at the sight of Lynx's open outrage. "So you're saying we're the shady planet that's bringing down the universe's property value?"

Lynx shrugged. "It's either that or they're all out there, no closer to finding us than we are them. Maybe all of us are held prisoner by our mortality, each of us only able to go as far away from our planets as our bodies allow." Lynx tilted his chin up and eyed the sky. "After all, there does seem to be one universal truth among all living organisms. We all die. Even the stars." Lynx dropped his chin and stared at Clint in a way that immediately took Clint's breath. Unexpectedly, Lynx turned shy, as if realizing how much passion he had shown on an odd subject. "I guess you think I'm pretty weird."

Clint shook his head. He couldn't let Lynx think

23

that. "You're one of a kind. A collector's edition. I'm lucky to have found you still in mint condition."

A snort escaped Lynx. He covered his mouth for a moment before shaking his head. His eyes danced with laughter. "Was that a nerd joke? I can't believe it." He shifted onto his knees and shuffled forward. Clint didn't hesitate to open his arms and let Lynx settle down between his thighs. With his back against Clint's chest, Lynx tilted his chin up and went back to staring at the stars. Clint couldn't stop staring at Lynx. "Clint Jones made a nerd joke," Lynx said, sounding like the idea filled him with wonder. "Imagine that."

Yep. Imagine that. Lynx changed him a little more every day. Clint could feel it happening and he refused to resist. He didn't know what his life would be like when Lynx was done with him. Whatever happened, Clint would be different at the end. That was exactly what Clint hoped for anyhow. He wanted to wake up one day and be a whole new person. One who didn't hurt other people because he was too weak to be real. Being with Lynx made him think that was possible. Clint held Lynx a little tighter. He couldn't wait to be a new man.

TWO

CONSIDERING LYNX HAD NEVER BEEN MUCH OF A drinker and he was a skinny guy, he was feeling a bit tipsy after four beers and an hour of staring at the night sky. He didn't notice how inebriated he was until they climbed down from the sundeck and headed inside Clint's house. He felt overly warm and a little dizzy. Lynx was a lot horny. Sitting between Clint's legs, smelling his cologne and feeling his huge muscles against him, Lynx was ready to pounce. He had already been on edge after their kiss. As he leaned against the kitchen counter, drinking a much-needed bottle of water while staring at Clint, Lynx broke. He wanted Clint to make a move, but he was always so stiff that Lynx didn't expect it would happen. That kiss earlier in the night was the closest Lynx had ever seen Clint come to spontaneity.

"You said I could ask you anything."

Clint didn't bat an eyelash. "I did. Was it a mistake?"

Lynx ignored his question and got straight to the point. "Why do you always seem so contained? It's almost like you're scared to lose control."

Clint's expression didn't as much as twitch. He was the same stoic and still waters as always.

Lynx shifted nervously, wondering if he was making a mistake. "It's in your eyes," Lynx explained, pushing on, because he couldn't stop. "You have a lot of fire, but it's like you have it in a chokehold. Why? Passion for life and creativity is what feeds my soul. You should be as intense as you want. Stop holding back. I want to hear all about what drives you."

"Are you ever quiet?"

At Clint's question, Lynx recognized he might have gone too far. He never knew where to draw the line. Lynx pressed his lips together, hoping to stifle the nonstop flow of words that always poured out. He fully realized Clint might have already answered if Lynx would only stop talking for half a second.

Sometimes, he wondered if he got on Clint's nerves with his nonstop moving and chatter.

Clint took a step closer. Lynx had to tilt his head back to keep holding his stare. While Lynx wasn't incredibly short, everyone was shorter than Clint. Clint always looked so intense. He made Lynx's stomach quiver. "I didn't say to stop. It was only a question." Clint's fingers swept through Lynx's Mohawk, sweeping it to one side. "I like the sound of your voice, but I worry your nonstop talking is a sign I make you nervous. I don't want that." Clint took another step. Their bodies were inches apart. Clint ducked his head. He was so close, Lynx could feel Clint's breath fanning across his cheek. Clint lowered his voice. "Or maybe I do," Clint admitted as he skimmed his lips across the line of Lynx's jaw.

Lynx fought the urge to fidget. All he had to do was turn his head and their lips would meet. He stared straight ahead, keeping his gaze locked on Clint's giant shoulder by will alone. "You didn't answer my question."

Clint leaned away just enough to meet Lynx's stare. Something dark flashed in Clint's eyes. "I can't trust myself enough to let go. When I'm passionate about anything, I'm obsessive and possessive.

Controlling. I don't want to be that person anymore, so I have to keep myself in check."

"If you don't want passion, why did you kiss me?" Lynx couldn't stop the question if he tried.

Clint smirked. Lynx's stomach twisted at the sight. This was the version of Clint he wanted. This Clint would fuck him hard. "You told me to think WWLD if I was uncomfortable. I did." Clint braced his hands on the counter on either side of Lynx, boxing him in, as if refusing let Lynx get away. "Are you upset I kissed you, knowing you're in love with Cage?"

A gut-check reaction had Lynx wincing. He hadn't known Clint knew that, but he didn't back down. "No. I wanted that kiss."

"Even though you're in love with Cage," Clint repeated, refusing to let Lynx hide.

Lynx mentally squared his shoulders. He wasn't ashamed of the unrequited love for his lifelong best friend. "Yes. Even though I love Cage, I still want you to kiss me." Lynx needed Clint to know he wanted more.

Clint didn't bite. "You've had years to win him. Why haven't you tried?"

"What makes you think I haven't? Maybe I've been trying unsuccessfully for countless years."

Clint shook his head. "I don't believe that. You're relentless and beautiful. I imagine he would've been helpless against you, if you'd been truly determined. So, why?"

"Because he was there," Lynx answered honestly. If Clint wanted all his truth, he would get it. "He was there when straight A's weren't good enough. He was there when being quiet, fitting in, and swallowing every dream I've ever had to make my father happy wasn't good enough. When I became valedictorian and got into MIT, Cage was there when that wasn't good enough." Lynx's voice grew stronger with the power of his inner rage and hurt. "And when I needed to break free from not being good enough and decided to decline college, Cage was the one who was there. He was the one who believed in me and my dreams, so much so that he invested the money he had gotten from literally having his life set on fire. Cage moved us here where living expenses were cheaper and bought us a place to live, put up all the money for Caged Lynx Games, and told me countless times how proud he is of me." Lynx took a breath, trying to squelch the pride and love in his heart for a man who would never love him back. His throat burned from the pain of never having who he wanted. Despite his best efforts,

Lynx's voice still shook with the power of his emotions. "So if Cage needs me to never love him so he can feel secure knowing I will never leave him alone in the darkness, then that's what he'll get. You have your answer, so you should definitely stop teasing and kiss me now."

Clint's eyes hooded, turning his stare sultry. His weight leaned slightly in, pinning Lynx in place. "Should I? You're making me think I should take you home instead, before I find myself living as your second choice."

Despite Clint's words, his actions didn't match. The air pulsed with barely constrained desire. Lynx's hands found Clint's waist. He towed the man closer. "We both know I'm not your first choice either. You'd much rather have whoever it is that has you keeping yourself restrained like a pressure cooker ready to blow." Lynx took a chance. He skimmed his fingertips across Clint's hips, following Clint's waistband until he reached the buckle of Clint's belt. He loosened it while boldly holding Clint's stare. "You don't scare me. I want you to blow." He slid Clint's zipper down. "In fact, I'm counting on you to make me hurt."

Clint's mouth slammed into his with so much force that Lynx tasted blood. Desperation clawed at

Lynx's insides and poured through their kiss. Lynx found himself clawing at Clint's shirt, trying to tear it from his body. No one had ever kissed Lynx like Clint—like if he didn't have Lynx, then he would die.

A sexy growl escaped Clint. Lynx's feet left the floor and the world tilted as Clint tossed Lynx over his shoulder. Lynx gasped for air as Clint ate up the floor between his kitchen and bedroom. Everything tilted again as Lynx found himself on his back with Clint's huge body on top of him. Air became secondary to the need to be closer. They kissed and fought to strip each other at the same time. It was madness and Lynx didn't care. There was fire and need pumping through his veins. He pulled Clint's hair and bit his bottom lip. In a flash of motion, Lynx was flipped onto his stomach. Rough hands squeezed his ass and probed at his asshole. Teeth sank into his back.

"Oh, god." The breathless cry was out of his control. His hard cock throbbed and leaked. He moved restlessly against the mattress seeking relief. He heard the crinkle of the condom wrapper. That was all the warning Lynx got. His knees were shoved apart and Clint thrust inside him in one solid stroke. A loud cry tore from Lynx's throat.

Clint took no mercy. He kissed and bit every place he could reach while fucking Lynx hard. "That's it, sexy," Clint praised as he pounded inside Lynx. "Take all of me." Lynx moaned and begged. Clint's fingers dug so hard into Lynx's skin, there would be bruises. "Let me hear your pleasure, Lynx. Don't hold back. You're so hot and tight. I knew you would be. You have no idea how many times I've pictured you like this." He thrust hard and made Lynx's eyes roll back in his head. "This asshole is mine. Tell me it's mine."

"It's yours," Lynx cried. It really was. Clint owned him in that moment. Lynx would have done anything, said anything for Clint to keep going.

Clint's fingers encircled Lynx's throat. He squeezed. It wasn't enough to cut off the oxygen. The pressure was only enough to let Lynx know who was in charge. Clint bit his earlobe and growled against his ear. "I'm going to be in this ass all night. Don't think once is enough to feed someone like me."

Fuck. Lynx needed that. With his eyes squeezed shut, Lynx swung wildly between gasping for air and grinding his back teeth. He was so close. Lynx didn't know if he would pop a blood vessel or come. His entire body strained almost painfully toward the abyss. Clint was so goddamn big in every way. Every time he thrust, his massive weight rocked Lynx against the mattress while he pounded at that internal button that had Lynx half insane. Lynx dug his fingers into the mattress and swallowed down his cries. Clint's fingers tightened on Lynx's throat, cutting off his oxygen. Lynx flew apart in a silent blast of ecstasy. His entire body shook.

A loud cry sounded against his shoulder as Clint rode Lynx's ass into orgasm. Pride filled Lynx's chest at the sound. He had done that. Possessiveness washed over him like a tsunami. He wanted to pull that sound from Clint again. Lynx wasn't done. Not by a long shot. He was addicted now. Clint would come again, even if it killed him.

THREE

STILL HALF ASLEEP, CLINT DROVE ON autopilot. While they had slept in, they hadn't slept long, and Clint's muscles ached in all the best ways. He was relaxed to the point of almost lethargic. Lynx seemed to be the same, since he was quiet for the first time ever. Clint might have worried if Lynx wasn't also holding his hand and stroking his arm. Each time Clint glanced his way, Lynx smiled sleepily at him. Clint would have been happy to stay in bed all day, but Lynx had work to do with Cage. He would take the man home and then go back to bed. Clint needed the rest if he hoped to pull a repeat performance tonight after the convention.

As Lynx's house came into view, Clint forced

himself to focus on it instead of Lynx. Lynx lived in a nice neighborhood. While his house was gorgeous, it was nothing anyone would suspect a man to own who also owned a multimillion-dollar company. It was a four-bedroom brick house with a two-car garage and the world's shortest driveway. Clint always found himself checking the back end of his truck to make sure he wasn't sticking out halfway in the road when he parked. It was odd to Clint that Lynx drove an old car and lived in a small house. In fact, other than his high-tech security and high-end home office, Lynx lived like a middle-class guy. Before now, Clint had never felt he had any right to ask why. Now he had been inside Lynx. Clint felt that gave him some liberties.

As he walked inside with Lynx, Clint decided to broach the topic. "I've always been curious. Why don't you live like most millionaires? Not that I'm complaining," he tacked on. Clint didn't want Lynx thinking Clint cared one way or the other.

Lynx emptied his pockets on the table by the door. He didn't look at Clint as he answered. "I was raised by people who live like millionaires. You know how that went." His chin lifted. Their gazes met. "Caged Lynx has never been about the money. It's about a dream. It's about offering kids and adults an alternate place to live when real life sucks ass." His mouth lifted in one corner. "I'm not hard to please. As long as I have a roof over my head, food to eat, and transportation, then all the rest is just icing."

"Mr. Lynx, your father is calling."

A smile tugged at Clint's lips. "I see you have the Charlie home system like Cage." It made sense for Cage to have a smart home system that ran his life, since Cage was blind. Of course, since Lynx had helped invent the system, Clint supposed it made sense for Lynx to have one as well, but the computer system calling Lynx Mr. Lynx was funny to Clint for some reason. Maybe he was just sleep-drunk.

Lynx pulled a face. "Poetic timing. You're about to get a front row seat to my distaste for millionaires. Charlie, put my father on speaker."

"Father on speaker," Charlie confirmed.

Lynx moved to sit on the large leather couch in the center of his living room. "Hola, Papa."

A loud sigh filled the room followed closely by a slight accent tinted with old-world haughtiness. "You would think I would be accustomed to your rude greetings by now."

Even though Lynx stared at nothing, he still

rolled his eyes. "Did you need something in particular, Papa?"

"I'm wondering if you've given any thought to my suggestion about selling your half of your little project to Cage so you can move home and take your rightful place with NewWay Robotics."

"I don't need to think about it. My little project and my life are here in Austin. NewWay doesn't need me. It has you."

"You're only saying that because you missed your chance at MIT. If you had gone to college, you would understand your place."

Lynx growled. "I didn't miss my chance," Lynx said, cutting his father off. "I chose not to go."

As Lynx's father's voice grew louder with anger, Clint eased toward the door. He wasn't sure he should stay. "I was trying to be diplomatic. Missing your chance sounds better than me saying you blew your entire future by following your cock to Texas. You've had plenty of time to play with your little friend. Now it's time to come home. Real men know when playtime ends and reality begins."

Clint moved away from the door and sat in the recliner by the couch. This lecture sounded oddly familiar. It was like his dad was alive again and in the room with them. Clint couldn't leave Lynx to deal with this alone.

"I am home."

"That dump you call a house isn't a home. It's a squatter's shack."

Lynx set his elbow on the arm of the couch and propped up his head with his hand. He settled in like he expected this to take a while. "Most people would love to have this house, and it's mine. Of course, that's what really bugs you about it. It's mine and I bought it with my money. There's nothing you can do or take away from me to make me toe your line. This conversation is boring. How's Mom?"

"She's in Belize. We're not talking about her. This is about you and your complete failure at life. It's time to stop humiliating yourself and us with these games you are making. You are dishonoring your family name. It is bad enough that you've created such violent trash for the youth of the world, but now I hear you have ventured into VR porn as well. I'm ashamed to say you are my son."

While Lynx didn't even flinch, Clint took it in the gut. No one should say such things to their child. People were supposed to love their children. While Clint's parents had sucked, they had never spoken to him like this. If every conversation had been like this throughout Lynx's life, there was no way Lynx had walked away unscarred. A spark of anger lit in Clint's chest.

Lynx's father kept talking. His insults grew bigger and cut deeper with every word. He left no topic untouched, from Lynx's sexuality to his friendship with a blind, scarred man. At least if he had to be gay, he could find a successful or beautiful man. Clint drew steady breaths, trying not to notice the way Lynx transformed. No longer was Lynx the brightest star in the room. His inner light dimmed as he withdrew further inside himself by the second. Every insult that ticked by, Clint watched Lynx die a little.

"I should have gone against your mother and sent you to an orphanage. We should have tried again for a real child."

Lynx rubbed his chest.

Something inside Clint snapped. "Charlie, hang up the phone." Clint half expected Charlie wouldn't obey commands from him. He had to try.

"Call disconnected."

Lynx stared straight ahead, emotionless. "I don't need you to save me."

Clint didn't doubt it. "I know."

"You shouldn't have intervened. Now he has more fodder for when he calls back."

Even though Lynx's words were delivered without an ounce of emotion, Clint could tell Lynx wasn't happy with him. He stood. Clint was good at overstaying his welcome. He recognized he needed to go. "I'm sorry. You're right. I shouldn't have done that. He was insulting you and I didn't like it, but it wasn't my place to get involved."

Lynx finally focused on him. He looked empty inside. "We're not dating. You have no reason to care about my feelings."

Clint fought hard to keep his expression blank. "Noted. Not dating." It didn't seem they were friends after all.

"Mr. Lynx, your father is calling."

Clint shook his head and moved for the door. "I'll let you get to that."

He made it to the door before Lynx spoke up. "Don't forget tonight's convention."

Clint kept his emotions under wraps. He had made a mistake showing Lynx his heart. "I have something else to do, but you have fun." Clint didn't look back or slow as he broke their plans. He had tried being different. Tried caring. That hadn't worked. He still destroyed everything. Clint had learned his lesson with Colt. When he felt too much, he was a ticking time bomb. He needed to walk away now, the way he hadn't with Colt. Lynx didn't care about him. Clint needed to accept that this time around and go. It was best for everyone, before Clint became someone he hated again.

"Why are you pouting?"

Lynx pulled his gaze away from Cage's bedroom floor and focused on Cage. Considering his best friend was blind, he didn't know how Cage would know he was sulking. Then again, Cage had known him all their lives. "I answered a call from a parental unit today."

Cage curled his nose. "Why would you do that to yourself?"

Lynx looked away. "Where's that adorable husband of yours?" They needed to change the subject. Lynx was too raw for this.

"Nope. Don't do that. Spill."

Lynx sighed. It was Cage. He couldn't deny him. Lynx could distract him, though. "I spent the night getting thoroughly fucked by Clint."

Cage shook his head. His shaggy blond hair

caught the light, distracting Lynx for a moment. Despite being badly scarred from being set on fire as a teenager, Cage was the most beautiful man in the world to Lynx. Clint was the sexiest. That thought froze Lynx's brain as an image of Clint's nude body filled his head. The air thickened.

"And sex with Clint made you talk to one of your parents, why? I don't see the connection. Was the D that bad or that good?"

A snort escaped Lynx without warning. Cage wasn't going to let this go. They knew each other with no secrets or embarrassment. Over the years, they had seen each other at their lowest and highest with every point in between. There was nothing they couldn't talk about. Lynx didn't know why he was hesitating now. Fuck it.

"The sex was off the charts—like eleven out of ten. So I guess I was feeling a bit too much when he brought me home this morning. My dad called while he was there, and I answered. Clint got a real look at me and I... I don't know."

"You withdrew so he wouldn't see how much your father's insults hurt," Cage surmised correctly.

"Yeah. That." Even Lynx heard the dejection in his voice. "We had plans to go to that wizard convention downtown again today. I ruined them."

Lynx leaned forward, getting into talking about things now that the gate opened. "I'm so pissed at myself, Cage. For the last few weeks, we've spent so much time together and I've been trying to coax him out of his shell. The moment he showed me the real him, I fucking shut him down. What's wrong with me? I really don't think it's purposeful self-destruction. Answering that call while Clint was there was all about letting him deeper into my life, and then I just slammed the door in his face. I know I'm not normal, but goddamn."

Cage found his usual chair and pulled it close. His sexy scent overcame Lynx. After almost thirty years of friendship, Lynx would have expected to be so used to Cage's presence that he no longer noticed his delicious smell, but no. Lynx always noticed.

Cage rubbed Lynx's arm. "I don't think it's all you, babe. From what I understand, Clint recently had his heart broken. I imagine he's still gun shy. It probably doesn't take much to push him away right now. But Clint strikes me as the type to respect straightforwardness, so that's my advice. Go see him. Be completely open and honest about why you did what you did and apologize. If he still pushes you away, then you know he's not worth beating yourself up about. It's better to find that out now, I should think."

"Hudson is home."

As the computer-generated announcement filled the air, a smile lit Cage's entire body. It was like he almost hovered in his chair in his euphoria. Lynx openly stared at Cage, studying his every reaction. He didn't jump to hide any of his scars. Instead, he kept his face turned toward the doorway, as if he could truly see. Lynx knew Cage saw Hudson with his heart. The backs of his eyes burned as he watched Cage visibly holding his breath, waiting for the love of his life to cross the threshold. Lynx had never felt lonelier than he did in that moment. He was so tired of pretending upbeat happiness to make other people smile.

"I'm going to go."

Cage's expression turned concerned again. "You don't have to leave."

Yes he did. "I know." He stood and forced his usual carefree mask back into place. "I have an apology to make."

Hudson cleared the door. "Hey, guys. Did I miss anything good?"

"I bought you wizard robes," Lynx said brightly.

Hudson was adorable. His big blue eyes fixed

upon Lynx. An adorable nose scrunch let Lynx know how Hudson felt about the idea. He was beautiful. Lynx wished he was beautiful too.

"What are wizard robes?" He moved to sit on Cage's lap as he questioned Lynx. Cage's arms wrapped around Hudson's waist. His lips found Hudson's throat.

An exasperated huff escaped Lynx. "You have no culture. There aren't enough hours in the day to catch you up on all the fandom you're missing. Cage, you're failing your husband if you don't make him watch at least three geek movies tonight. That's your homework. Then I expect an apology for the lack of enthusiasm for your gift."

"Mmmm," Cage hummed against the side of Hudson's neck. "What do you say, beautiful? A night curled up together. You watching movies and me focusing on you."

Lynx threw his hands up in defeat. "I give up. You know dang well that you won't watch any movies with Cage's horny hands all over you. I'm going. You two have fun. I'm not jealous," Lynx yelled over his shoulder as he headed for the door. He wasn't, Lynx realized as he jogged down the stairs. Not about Cage loving Hudson anyway. Maybe he was a little envious of their love in general

—like he wanted to be loved too—but he was happy for Cage. It was obvious Hudson truly loved him. They were the real deal. Hudson made Lynx feel like Cage was finally settled and didn't need Lynx anymore. Lynx rubbed his chest. His job was done. Lynx was done.

FOUR

While swinging wildly between self-hatred and nervousness, Clint headed inside the nearly empty diner. Raiden was easy to spot. Not only had Clint studied the guy's picture on the Cubs for Rent website, he was also the only person sitting alone. Of Asian descent with bleach blond hair, Raiden was a rare beauty. His sweet light brown eyes swept Clint's way as Clint reached the table. His full lips turned upward into a sexy smile. Clint felt like a fucking idiot. Never in a million years would Clint have expected to pay someone to have dinner with him. Insanity.

"Hey," Raiden said, sounding oddly excited. "You look exactly how you sounded on the phone."

Clint didn't know why, but the claim pulled a

smile from him. He slid into the booth across from Raiden. "I saw your picture, so I can't answer in kind."

Raiden chuckled. It was a sultry sound. His eyes danced with good humor—like he was a nice person. Clint's shoulders relaxed as some tension drained from him. Before either of them could speak, a waitress appeared at the edge of their table. "What can I get you two to drink?"

They spent a second ordering. Once they were alone, Raiden focused on him once more. "So, tell me about yourself, cowboy."

Clint swiped his hands nervously on his thighs. "There's not much to tell. I'm thirty-eight and retired. My life is pretty unexciting. Why don't you tell me about yourself instead?"

Raiden sat straighter, as if facing an inquisition. "What would you like to know?"

Clint shrugged. "Whatever. How did you end up working for Cubs for Rent? What do you like to do? Anything. I'm not picky. I like hearing people talk." A lump formed in Clint's throat as he made the confession. His ears rang every second he spent without Lynx and his nonstop chatter.

For a moment, Raiden pressed his lips together and hummed, as if searching for a place to start. He gazed at the corner for a second before he focused on Clint again with a smile. "Okay. Maybe I'll just start at the very beginning. I have eleven brothers and sisters."

"Whoa."

"Right," Raiden said with a chuckle. "We grew up in a house with two bathrooms and one of those my parents kept for only them, so I'm used to fighting for stuff. The second I turned eighteen, I got out. I wasn't even out of high school yet. A friend from work had an apartment and said I could crash there until I graduated as long as I drove them to work and paid two hundred a month. It sounded like heaven to me. Of course, I had no idea how expensive it is to live. I floated from one horrible roommate to the next until I realized I had to find a way to make more money so I could live alone." His hands lifted and fell as he spoke, drawing Clint's gaze their way. They were small and feminine like the rest of Raiden. Clint would break him. He forced his gaze back to Raiden's face and made himself pay attention to his words. This was only a dinner date. "One night, I was waitressing at this fancy restaurant." Clint smiled at Raiden's choice of words. "And there was this couple at one of my tables. One guy was probably seventy and the other guy was maybe twenty, but they kept openly flirting with each other. I was fascinated. The young guy was personable as hell. I found myself hanging out at their table way longer than necessary, chatting with them both. It finally dawned on me that both men were flirting with me. I made myself scarce after that. When they left, the older gentleman left me a huge tip and his number written on the back of a Cubs for Rent card. The younger guy slipped his phone number to me through another waitress. It was written on the back of a Cubs for Rent card." Raiden's smile was captivating. He looked like he was a genuinely happy person. Clint wondered what that must be like.

"Did you call either man or just the company?"

At Clint's question, Raiden laughed and blushed. "The older man's card also had a very lucrative offer if I made their party of two a party of three for the night." Raiden's blush deepened.

Clint had to know. His cheeks ached, making him realize he was smiling hard. "Did you accept?"

Everything about Raiden vibrated with his open embarrassment. "Maybe."

A loud laugh burst from Clint. He pressed his lips together as heads turned their way. He laughed way less than he ever smiled, but Raiden was brave.

Clint wasn't sure he would have the balls to confess what Raiden had. "Tell me more."

Raiden's embarrassment turned to genuine laughter at Clint's demand. The air shifted between them. They felt like friends. Clint's chest eased. Pressure he hadn't known was suffocating him until it was gone left him. He took a cleansing breath. This date was exactly what he needed. They took turns talking. The sky got darker outside the window. Clint's phone buzzed a few times. He ignored it. No one would seek him out in an emergency, and he wouldn't be rude. Raiden possessed a special talent for prying words from Clint. He swore his throat hurt from talking. Clint hadn't used his voice so much in years.

Clint straightened in his seat and his back popped, making him realize how long he had sat in the same spot. He glanced around. The place was dead. "Damn. I'll have to leave our server a huge tip for keeping her table hostage all night."

Raiden glanced at his watch. "Wow. Yeah. I can't believe how long we've been here. I didn't realize it had gotten so late."

After digging out a few bills, Clint tossed them on the table and focused on Raiden. "Where are you parked? I'll walk you to your car."

Raiden slid from the booth at the same time as Clint. "Out back," he said as they both came to their feet.

Shock had Clint missing a beat. Raiden was nearly as tall as him. That was rare. Clint was used to staring down at people. Raiden was all legs. Clint understood why people paid to be with him.

Clint motioned for the door. "After you."

Raiden flashed him a sexy smile and headed for the door. Clint let his gaze slide down Raiden's body. He was honest enough to admit he had chosen Raiden because he reminded Clint of Lynx. Now that they'd gotten to know each other, Clint realized their similarities were in looks alone. Lynx was nerdy and cared nothing about his looks. Raiden was feminine and obviously took great care to look perfect. Honestly, Raiden wasn't Clint's type at all. Yet Clint had genuinely had an amazing time tonight. He found himself setting his hand on the small of Raiden's back as they stepped outside and fell into step beside each other. They didn't speak on the way to Raiden's car.

Raiden motioned toward a black Honda C-RV. "This is me. Thank you for dinner."

Clint nodded. "It was nice. Thank you for agreeing to join me."

Raiden turned and faced him. His gaze moved over Clint's face, as if searching for something. "I'm off the clock now."

"Okay." Clint's usual state of discomfort came roaring back. "You're the first person I've ever hired to go out with me, so I don't really know how all this works. Was that your way of telling me to get lost?"

A bright smile lit Raiden's face. "No. For legal reasons, I was being extremely clear that you're no longer paying me." He took a step closer. "So there are no misunderstandings when I do this." His hands slid across Clint's hips as he shuffled closer. Raiden's lips touched his.

Clint stopped breathing. Everything about Raiden felt soft and feminine. It was disconcerting. He was scared to hurt the guy. Then Raiden bit his bottom lip and Clint was onboard. He found himself backing Raiden against the door of his SUV. As their bodies melded, Raiden felt like every bit the man he was while going hard against Clint's body. It wasn't the desperate kiss that he had come to expect from Lynx. Instead, this was skilled. The idea had Clint backing away a hair, slowing things down. He didn't relish the idea of being just another guy to anyone.

Raiden pulled away. He looked turned on. "Call

me directly next time. I'd love to go out for real, if you're interested."

Clint nodded. He was interested. "I'll call."

The way Raiden smirked made Clint wish he didn't think so much. He probably could have taken Raiden to bed tonight, if he had tried. He promised himself he would next time. After all, he needed to meet new people. Start a new life.

"Be careful going home."

At his words, Raiden's smile turned sweet. "You too."

Clint backed away and watched until Raiden was safely locked inside his vehicle before walking away. It had been an odd night... in a good way. Clint would work harder at getting to know new people, he decided as he climbed behind the wheel of his truck. One of his biggest failures was putting too much of his heart into one person at a time while no one else did the same for him. Even Colt hadn't been focused solely on him and that was one of the many reasons Clint had turned into such a controlling bastard when they were together. Clint had issues and Colt had never stopped dating other people. The harder Colt fought to break free of him, the tighter Clint held on, finding more and more ways to own him. Sometimes, Clint thought he had gone half crazy when he had been with Colt. He didn't even recognize who he had been back then. That person scared him a little. Made him realize how far he would go. It was terrifying. That was why he had to let Lynx be free of him. He could already see Lynx struggling to stay independent and draw lines. So Clint would respect that and move on before he went crazy again. That was what was best for everyone involved. That was best for Clint.

* * *

IT WAS POSSIBLE LYNX SHOULD JUST GO HOME. Clint wasn't home and he was avoiding Lynx's texts. For some strange reason, Lynx couldn't force himself to move from his spot, sitting on his trunk, leaned back against the back window, and staring at the stars. This really was a great place. Clint's cabin in the middle of the woods on the edge of Lake Travis was gorgeous. It wasn't too big or too small. It was perfect. He knew from Clint's various comments that he had done something horrible to the man he loved, losing him permanently. But really, Lynx didn't understand why no one had snapped him up. He was one hell of a catch. It was possible he was way too quiet for some people's tastes. Clint didn't talk about himself or offer any insights at all unless they were dragged from him. Truth be told, Lynx didn't know that much about Clint either. He knew the guy had money from horse racing and the family ranch he had sold. Clint didn't need Lynx or his money. In fact, Clint had no reason to hang around him at all.

The thing was, Lynx made people tired. He talked too much and moved too much. Lynx paced and jumped topics. He was hyperactive and obsessive about ridiculous topics. Clint was the first person Lynx had met besides Cage who seemed to like him as is. If Lynx got in his car and left now, he might never know if that meant something. Plus, he really liked Clint. Lynx didn't want to lose him.

The sound of a car caught Lynx's attention. He tilted his chin down as headlights turned down the driveway. Lynx forced himself to sit up as Clint steered his truck into the spot beside Lynx's car. Clint's expression was completely closed as he stepped from his truck. All the passion Clint had shown the night before was gone. He was back to being contained. Hiding.

Lynx didn't give him time to ask why Lynx was sitting in his driveway. "I'm sorry."

Clint seemed genuinely surprised. His eyebrows rose. "Why?"

Some of Lynx's bravery faltered in the face of so much. In that moment, he felt like everything he did and had done was wrong. "For me, I guess. For all the times I've made you do things I knew you didn't want to do. I'm sorry I'm not quiet or still or particularly grounded. Most of all, I'm sorry for being a dick this morning when you were trying to help. You deserve a better friend than me."

"You don't have to apologize," Clint said with a shake of his head. "I'm a temporary person. I know that."

Lynx's brows snapped together. "A temporary person. What in the hell is that supposed to mean?"

Clint made a helpless motion. "I'm just that guy. The one who is disposable, I guess. When people are done playing whatever role they're playing with me, they move along. It's not your fault. It's me. I'm just not worth keeping around or whatever."

The immediate punch to the gut had Lynx pressing his hand to his stomach. It was soul wrenching that Clint believed he meant nothing to Lynx. "You're not some fleeting part of my life. If you haven't noticed, I tend to keep people forever. People aren't replaceable to me. Hell, you've seen how my dad treats me and I haven't booted him yet. Although I did block his number after you left, but that's another story. You're not temporary to me by any definition of the word."

"I'm pretty sure there's only one definition of the word," Clint said, still stone-faced.

Lynx huffed. "There's two definitions. One is the lasting thing and then there's the office worker thing. Damn near every word has more than one definition, even if it's only so the dictionary can be—"

"I love that you talk nonstop."

"Superfluous," Lynx said, finishing his thought even though his mind broke at Clint's confession.

"Did you call me superfluous?"

Lynx made a dismissive motion. "I was talking about the dictionary. You like that I talk nonstop?"

Clint gave him a sharp nod. "You make me feel less alone when I'm listening to you talk."

It was hard, but Lynx managed not to smile like an idiot. "I'm glad you like to listen to me, because I have a lot to say about you not going to the con with me today. I don't know if you noticed, but wizard robes aren't cheap, especially considering you only get to wear them in public once—"

"I went on a date," Clint said, interrupting Lynx.

Like that, Lynx's temper snapped. "Well,

maybe that's exactly why you're temporary to people." Lynx headed for his car without looking back. Fuck this. He couldn't believe Clint fucked him last night and then took someone else out the next. To hell with that bullshit. Before Lynx could get in his car, Clint overcame him. Lynx's chest hit his driver's side door as Clint molded against his back, stopping him from getting away.

"You said we aren't dating."

Lynx tapped the roof of his car in his frustration. "So you immediately go fuck someone else. That's good to know."

A sexy rumble of laughter vibrated against his ear as Clint kissed him below his earlobe. "It's ten o'clock. What time did you get home after a night with me? We had dinner." He licked Lynx's pulse point. "I chose him because he looks like you."

Lynx growled, refusing to be swayed by Clint's kisses. "No one looks like me." Chill bumps rose on his skin as Clint sucked on his neck. "I'm one of a fucking kind."

"His parents are Chinese immigrants."

Lynx stamped his foot. "My dad is from *Japan* and my mom is white."

Another sexy chuckle vibrated against his skin.

"I should take more men on dates. You're even sexier when you're jealous."

Outrage had Lynx balling up his fist and blindly punching behind him. He aimed downward, hoping for a good hit to the junk. Instead, he worried he had broken his pinky when his hand collided with whatever Clint had in his pocket. He cried out in pain, but it sounded like pleasure as Clint boldly cupped Lynx's erection through his jeans, proving—despite his anger—Clint still turned him on.

Clint massaged, making Lynx's eyes fall closed and his head fall forward. A moan vibrated in his throat. Clint made quick work of his clothes. Lynx couldn't do anything but writhe in Clint's arms as Clint's fingers encircled Lynx's cock. "This is one of the great things about living in the middle of nowhere. I could fuck you right here."

"Go to hell. I don't know where your body has been tonight."

Clint's teeth sank into Lynx's shoulder, punishing Lynx for his sassiness. "You said we're not dating."

Lynx sniffed but didn't respond.

The hold on Lynx's cock tightened. Clint moved against his back, letting Lynx feel how hard Clint was for him. "Admit we're dating."

In an act of defiance, Lynx pressed his lips together.

Clint's fingers encircled Lynx's throat. He tugged, urging Lynx's head back against his chest. Clint pumped faster at Lynx's erection while gently squeezing his throat. "Say it, Lynx. Tell me we're dating."

Lynx squeezed his eyes shut and fought the growing pleasure. Clint had gone out with someone else. Technically, it was Lynx's fault for pushing him away, but Lynx wouldn't tolerate Clint doing that again. Fuck. They were dating. Clint went still, stealing any chance of orgasm.

Clint's voice sounded deadly as he spoke against Lynx's ear. "Admit we're dating, or you can go somewhere else for this. I'm not your toy."

"We're dating."

In a flash, Clint spun Lynx in his arms. His mouth came down hard on Lynx's. Their tongues fought for dominance as Clint stroked Lynx hard and fast. Insanity clawed at Lynx's brain as he shamelessly rode Clint's palm. As his orgasm hit, Clint gasped as if the pleasure had been his. He didn't stop stroking Lynx, letting Lynx's cum soak his clothes, as if it was his prize for blowing Lynx's mind.

Clint's kiss turned sweet. Something shifted in Lynx's chest. He was vulnerable in the aftermath of Clint. Lynx cared too much. "You're not allowed to date anyone else," Lynx said between kisses.

He felt Clint smile against his lips. "You either."

"Agreed." Lynx loosened Clint's belt. He sucked Clint's bottom lip because he needed to taste it. In fact, he craved all of Clint's flavor. The second he set Clint's erection free, Lynx dropped to his knees. A loud gasp filled the air as Lynx licked Clint's length. Lynx didn't think he was especially good at giving head. He also wasn't one of those who couldn't wait to suck some guy's dick. There was something about Clint. He didn't know if it was the way Clint refused to let loose until Lynx pushed him, or if Lynx needed to mark his territory. Whatever the reason, Lynx needed to make Clint addicted.

Lynx put his heart into blowing Clint. He licked and sucked, growing bolder with each noise Clint made. He knew there would be bruises on his knees. Lynx also recognized Clint had probably enjoyed better service from hotter men. None of that mattered. He would make Clint happy. Clint openly fucked Lynx's mouth. His gasps and moans grew frantic. Lynx's eyes flipped upward. Clint stared down at him. He looked at Lynx like Lynx was the only man he wanted. Like Lynx had everything he craved. Lynx had never felt more powerful. Something filled him, trying to burst from his chest. He had never felt this way before. Lynx wanted more. Clint tilted his chin up and made a sound that stole Lynx's breath. He yanked Lynx from his knees. Hot cum hit Lynx on the way up. He didn't care. Lynx wanted Clint's cum drenching his body. Clint kissed him so hard and deep that Lynx had to fight for air. Then he felt it. As Lynx's arms encircled Clint's neck, he felt the way Clint trembled. Lynx's nose and eyes stung. He had done that. Clint shook for him. Oxygen mattered not at all in the face of their potential.

Clint's kiss softened until he pulled away and touched his forehead to Lynx's. They stared into each other's eyes. "I have a confession."

Lynx bit back a groan. Clint's confessions were a mixed bag tonight. "Okay."

"That was my first blow job."

Lynx blinked. "Shut up. You're thirty-eight. There's no fucking way."

He felt more than saw Clint's shrug. "I don't think I inspire people to want to pleasure me."

Lynx bit his bottom lip, fighting a smile. He wanted to hate how much Clint's words pleased him.

It shouldn't make him happy that no one had treated Clint the way Lynx did. The thing was, Lynx wanted to be special to Clint. He wanted to be more than anyone else had ever been to him.

Lynx buried his fingers in Clint's hair and held on. "I want your pleasure. I want all of you."

Clint's lips lightly brushed his again. "Stay."

Lynx nodded. He wasn't going anywhere. He wasn't finished with Clint yet.

It was odd how different Lynx was the minute his eyes closed. Clint imagined Lynx slept like the dead due to the massive energy he spent all day every day. When Lynx closed his eyes, he went from a massive ball of energy to complete stillness in an instant. He didn't snore or move. It was like a switch was flipped and he was out. He was beautiful. Clint couldn't stop staring at him. Looking at Lynx made Clint think about things he never had before. He didn't think he had ever noticed anyone's skin, but Lynx's was perfect. Lynx was a flawless wild child. Most people might not even notice Lynx, if not for his multi-colored hair and green eyes. Those two things made Lynx unique. But now that Clint had spent so much time with Lynx, he saw all the nuances others missed. He had gorgeous lips. They weren't so full they were distracting, but Clint had tasted them. They were pretty amazing.

Lynx had shown up to apologize. Clint couldn't get past that. No one had ever sought him out, fighting to keep him. He felt... warm all over—like special or whatever. Then, topping off an apology that Clint wasn't sure he deserved, Lynx had dropped to his knees in the middle of Clint's driveway. Lynx would definitely have bruises after that one. Honestly, Clint wasn't worth any of that, especially since he had gone out with Raiden tonight.

Clint found his hand sliding across Lynx's stomach. Lynx smiled in his sleep. Clint's heart squeezed in his chest. He felt... something. With no real plan, he scooted closer.

"Do you ever sleep?"

The groggy question had Clint smiling. "It's hard to close my eyes against the sight of you."

"I believe in you."

A chuckle slipped out at Lynx's words. "Is that convention thing still going on tomorrow?"

Lynx didn't answer right away. Clint tried to be still in case he had fallen back asleep. When he finally answered, his words were slurred like he was barely clinging to consciousness. "For a few hours."

"Good. I want to go."

"You're amazing."

Clint's throat swelled at the compliment. He wasn't amazing. Not even a little. Still, Clint needed Lynx to keep believing. "I will be. You'll see," Clint whispered, knowing Lynx was out again. Clint might be Lynx's second choice, but Lynx was Clint's second chance. He wouldn't squander it.

FIVE

Lynx stayed. There was no other way he could explain it. Clint had asked him to stay, and while Lynx was certain Clint meant that one night, Lynx had stayed. They got up every day and went about whatever they needed to do, and Lynx came home to Clint. If he ran late, Clint would text him, wanting to know when he would be home. That was the exact word he used every time—home. Somehow, Lynx ended up with a drawer and then a closet. They never talked about it. Lynx didn't give up his house. Clint didn't ask him to move in. Things just were the way they were. Three months into Lynx staying, they were a real couple.

Each day that passed without Lynx speaking to his parents, Lynx felt a little lighter. At some point, the only opinion that mattered became Clint's. Clint was the only voice in his head he heard. Lynx also became better at delegating. Since Cage and he no longer needed the constant distraction of work, he had let some things go, finally allowing some employees to take over most of their workload. Lynx might have worried he was on Clint's nerves by always being under his feet, if not for times likes now.

"One hint," Lynx begged. "I just need one hint about where we're going, and I'll be okay. You know I have anxiety."

Clint tore his eyes away from the road long enough to shoot Lynx a disbelieving look. "You don't have anxiety. You have impatience and you're spoiled. I have faith you can make it five more minutes."

That was all true. Clint spoiled the hell out of him, and Lynx had never possessed an ounce of patience. That didn't mean he wouldn't pout. He was like a kid when it came to surprises; Lynx wanted to know. Before he broke and asked again, Clint turned down a winding driveway. A huge red barn and fenced fields were the only things in sight.

"What is this place?"

"It's the only part of my family's land I didn't sell."

"Oh." It was pretty. That still didn't explain why Clint had marched him out to the truck and told him to get in if he wanted a surprise.

Clint parked near the barn's huge door and killed the engine. He slid out. "Come on."

Lynx followed.

Clint waited at the front of the truck. Their fingers automatically linked as they reached for each other at the same time. Side by side, they headed inside. Lynx tried looking in every direction. Everything smelled like hay, fresh air, and animal feces. The scraping of hooves and snorting of horses reached Lynx's ears before he spotted the first giant beast. He was solid black and humongous. Terrifying. Lynx stepped closer to Clint's side.

Clint chuckled. "You're not scared of horses, are you?"

Lynx shook his head. "I've just never been this close to one." Or seen one in real life, Lynx silently added. "I didn't realize they were so big."

Clint reached out and patted the beast's head before rubbing his nose. "Most aren't quite this big. Mercury is a Shire. They're the biggest horses in the world. He's been my baby since I turned eighteen."

Lynx blinked. "Horses live that long?"

Even Clint's snort was sexy. "Did you just call me old?"

Lynx shook his head. "I just didn't realize horses live that long."

Clint nodded and gave the horse more affection. "He's probably got another ten years in him. Don't you, boy?"

Mercury stamped his foot and Lynx swore the horse nodded. A smile pulled at the corners of Lynx's mouth. The horse did look smarter than most animals he had met. He found himself petting Mercury. He wasn't soft, but he also didn't kill Lynx, so there was that.

"Are you ready to meet your horse?"

Lynx's gaze shot to Clint. "What?"

A gorgeous smile stretched Clint's lips. "This beast needs to be ridden, and you can't let me ride alone."

"I can't ride a horse." Lynx hadn't meant to sound so horrified, but Mercury was huge. Lynx had no idea how to get on a horse so tall, and if he fell, it was over.

Clint wasn't tolerating any cowardice. "You can learn. I believe in you."

Even though Lynx didn't argue, he had no

intention of entrusting his life to an animal. Clint led him to another stall. A much smaller tan-colored horse came into view. It had curly hair—like a fluffy dog. Lynx's insides melted. "Oh my god. Look at you. You're freaking adorable."

"Just like his owner," Clint said with a chuckle. "Meet Jupiter. He's yours, if you want him."

Jupiter was not only beautiful; he was crazy friendly. He nosed at Lynx's hands, begging for pets. When Lynx rubbed his face and back, Jupiter danced in place. An irresistible desire to ride him overcame Lynx. "He's so awesome." Lynx tore his gaze away from Jupiter and focused on Clint. "Thank you. I really love him."

The contained version of Clint was back. Lynx had to take a slow breath. He always knew when Clint fought his nature, trying not to fall on Lynx like a man possessed. Before Clint, Lynx had never felt so desirable.

"He needs to be ridden."

"Does he?" Lynx never broke eye contact as he asked the question.

The way Clint smirked let Lynx know he hadn't missed the thinly veiled innuendo. "I'll teach you everything you need to know."

With one tiny nod from Lynx, Clint had Jupiter

saddled. He led Jupiter from the stall and into the field. Mercury tried to kick down his door as they passed.

Clint chuckled. "He's jealous."

Once they were in an open area, Clint showed Lynx how to mount his horse and how to control him. With a breath for courage, Lynx shoved his foot in the stirrup and swung his leg over Jupiter. It was easier than he expected. To his surprise, the horse obeyed every tug of the reins. Clint never left his side. After about an hour of practice, Lynx dismounted, feeling pretty confident. Clint made him lead the horse back to its stall and remove the saddle. It was a hell of a lot harder and heavier than Lynx expected.

"We'll work on it," Clint said, staying patient with him. "Come on." He motioned for Lynx to follow once they had Jupiter settled. Mercury kicked at the door again as they approached. "All right, monster. I'm coming." Clint opened the stall door and let Mercury out. Lynx swore he kept getting bigger. Clint was a big guy, so Lynx imagined he wasn't intimidated, but Lynx was.

Clint tossed a thick and scratchy-looking blanket —like the one that had been beneath Jupiter's saddle —across Mercury's back. He led Mercury to an overturned bucket. In one smooth motion, Clint stepped one foot on the bucket and leapt onto the horse's back. "He doesn't like a saddle," Clint explained as he easily controlled Mercury keeping him in place. "Come here, sexy."

Lynx eased closer.

"Put one foot on the bucket," Clint ordered. When he complied, Clint scooted back even as he reached down, grabbed Lynx's arm, and pulled him onto the horse in front of him. Clint always blew him away with his strength. If he hadn't been sitting cradled in Clint's arms, Lynx would have been completely terrified. Mercury was nothing like Jupiter. He felt wild—like he might do anything any second.

Clint kissed Lynx's ear as he led them slowly outside. "Hang on." That was all the warning Lynx got before they were off. At first, it was awful. His teeth rattled from the impact. Once Mercury hit his stride, the ride smoothed. His eyes watered from the wind whipping past them. Lynx was more than ninety percent sure that Clint was the only thing keeping him from flying off. Of course, judging by the burning in his thighs, he was also squeezing the life from Mercury. As a flowing river came into view, Clint tugged on the reins, slowing Mercury to a walk. The horse released loud, heaving breaths and shook his head but obeyed. They moved slow, following the bank's line. Clint held the reins in one hand while he kept his other arm wrapped around Lynx's waist. Lynx was more at peace than he could recall.

"What do you think of this place?"

Lynx thought it was heaven while sitting in Clint's hold. "It's beautiful."

"Do you think you could live here?"

"There's no house, so probably not. I'm not an outdoorsman, if you haven't noticed."

Clint didn't laugh the way Lynx hoped. "What if I built you a house?"

Lynx tried looking over his shoulder to see Clint's expression. He couldn't twist enough in their current position to get a good look at Clint's face. "Is that your way of asking me to live with you?"

Clint didn't answer. "If you'd rather stay at the cabin, that's fine. When I had a huge house on this land, I hated the place. Everywhere I looked, I saw my crappy childhood. But lately, I've been kind of missing this part of farm life. It's no big deal to pay someone to care for the horses, but sometimes I miss it. You've made me feel like I finally have the real family that deserves this land."

74

Lynx chuckled even as he melted. "So you're just going to act like I didn't ask you a question just now. Okay."

Clint pressed his lips to Lynx's shoulder. "You know I'm not good with words." Before Lynx could demand he try, Clint cut him off. "I wasn't asking you to move in."

"Oh." Lynx didn't think he did a very good job at hiding his disappointment.

"I thought we were already living together."

Lynx perked up. "Oh. I guess—"

"I was asking you to marry me."

All sense and ability to speak left Lynx. He hadn't thought they were there yet. Clint hadn't said he loved Lynx or anything even close to that. While Lynx hadn't said the words either, he definitely felt them. The thing was, Lynx still wasn't sure he was really good enough for Clint.

"I don't think I've ever seen you speechless. Unfortunately, I'm pretty sure it's not a good thing."

"Just give me a minute. I'm taking it in."

Clint's lips skimmed the shell of his ear. "Okay."

Could he marry someone who didn't love him? Clint was beyond good to him. They were sexually compatible. Not only did they never fight, they never as much as snipped at each other. It was a good life.

Even if Clint didn't love him, he still treated Lynx better than Lynx's parents ever had. The big question was, could Lynx live the rest of his life knowing he wasn't really who Clint wanted. He was who Clint had settled for, and Lynx wasn't sure he cared. Being settled for was better than not being noticed at all, which was his usual state.

"If you're trying to think of a way to say no without hurting me—"

"No," Lynx said, rushing to reassure Clint. "I'm not trying to think of a way to say no. I'm trying to calm down before I say yes."

Clint pulled Mercury to a stop. His arms tightened around Lynx, hugging him against his chest and squeezing the air from his lungs. "I'll make you happy," Clint said quietly against Lynx's ear.

Lynx didn't doubt him. While it wasn't some huge proclamation of love, Lynx recognized this proposal had been very Clint-like. He had given Lynx a horse and laid out solid reasoning for them to be married while showing him how much he had to offer. At the end of the day, Lynx didn't need a horse or for Clint to build him a house, but Lynx did need Clint. He wanted the family Clint claimed they would be. Being with Clint was already more like love than he had ever had before. At the end of the day, Lynx felt like he had to bet everything on Clint. Otherwise, he would always wonder what could have been.

———

ON THE SLOW RIDE BACK TO THE BARN, CLINT listened to Lynx chattering with a happy hum in his chest. He hadn't really expected Lynx to say yes. In fact, he had been so certain Lynx would say no that he hadn't gone through with his original plan to get down on one knee at a gorgeous spot by the river. Now he had another memory to file away where he wasn't brave when he wanted to be.

As Lynx waited for Clint to finish brushing down Mercury's coat, he massaged his thighs. "Jesus, this is going to take some practice. I have a feeling I'll be walking funny tomorrow."

Clint couldn't fight his laughter as he left Mercury behind and headed for the truck. "I could put the nail in that coffin."

"Another joke from Clint Jones. One of these days, I'll have a comedian on my hands. Oh, should I take your last name? Can you imagine when I meet new people? My amazing skin tone with the name Lynx Jones. Everyone will think I'm adopted." The laughter flashing in Lynx's eyes was irresistible, but the thing that literally took Clint down to one knee was the sound of Lynx using his last name. Lynx stared down at him. "You know you're too tall when I still don't have to look that far down when you're on your knees. Why are you on your knees anyhow?"

Clint dug out the ring he had bought two weeks ago. His heart had been in his throat ever since. "This is what I meant to do. Will you marry me?"

Lynx blinked fast—like his brain fried. "Damn. You really meant to do this. It wasn't a spur-of-the-moment decision."

Clint's face hurt from smiling. "I really meant to do this. I know it's only been a few months, but I know my mind." He took a breath. "I know what I want." Lynx. Forever.

After a moment passed, Lynx startled slightly. "Oh, are you waiting for me to say yes again? Yes. Of course. This is what I want too."

Clint slipped the ring on Lynx's finger. It fit perfectly, as he knew it would since he had tested it out during one of Lynx's death sleeps. He came to his feet. While Lynx stared at the ring, Clint stared at him. He looked free from doubts. Even though Clint knew he wasn't the man Lynx had hoped to one day marry, Clint wouldn't let Lynx regret him.

They didn't have to rush out and get married tomorrow. Hopefully, one day, Lynx would love him, and Clint wouldn't have to choke on the words anymore.

Lynx's gaze lifted and collided with his. Clint swore he saw something in Lynx in that moment. A spark of... something. "Being with you is the best thing I've ever done for myself."

Clint would take it. It wasn't the "I love you" he wanted, but it was close enough. Clint shuffled closer. Lynx did too. When their lips met, Clint's breath left him. He cupped Lynx's face and deepened their kiss. He backed away before things got too heated. Lynx kept Clint hard. Sometimes, he had to fight the urge to do more than find the closest flat surface. Clint quickly turned away before Lynx could see his hunger. He snagged the small ice chest and blanket he had shoved behind the seats when Lynx wasn't looking before they left the house.

Lynx chuckled when he saw what Clint held. "Wow. You thought of everything."

Clint winked and headed for a nearby tree. He spread out the blanket in the shade and moved the cooler to hold down one corner.

Clint sat and patted his thighs. "Right here, gorgeous. The most comfortable seat in the house."

A sexy smile stretched Lynx's lips as he straddled Clint. His arms snaked around Clint's neck. Lynx's eyes flashed with happiness as he settled himself on Clint's lap. Their lips brushed again. Clint was beginning to think he wouldn't win the battle against his lust. Lynx shoved, sending him sprawling onto his back. In his usual childlike enthusiasm, Lynx bounced a little as he stared down at Clint, making things worse... and harder.

"Oh, guess what?"

Clint settled in. He massaged Lynx's thighs. "What?"

Like always, that was all it took for Lynx to be off, talking faster than Clint could keep up sometimes. "There's this huge convention that takes place every year in Vegas. It's like the usual con, but much bigger, and that's where the hottest new games releasing over the next year are announced. I always attend. Anyhow, this year, we're hosting a mega party to market our new wizard game releasing on Black Friday. There's also an award ceremony going on at the same time. It's where they award the best games of the year and whatnot. I hadn't really worried about the awards being held at the same time as the party because, while Cage and I are a huge corporation, we're still much smaller than the big dogs, and they always win everything with their first-person shooter shit. I mean, it's not like free roam puzzle games and sex-themed VR games can compete against that."

"Sex games. I'm in."

Lynx ignored him. "Anyhow, I figured most people would rather attend a party than some boring awards, but I just found out that Caged Lynx Games is up for developer of the year. How fucking fantastic is that? I mean, we don't stand a chance of winning, but that's still fucking amazing to me."

"I'm so proud of you." Clint meant the words from the bottom of his soul. He thought Lynx was amazing.

Lynx went silent. He stared down at Clint with his heart in his eyes. "Really?"

"Of course. You risked everything to follow your dreams, and look at you now. Thousands of people have jobs because of you. You touch countless people's lives every day and they don't even realize it. You're in their homes and giving them an escape. That award is yours whether they give it to you or not. You're amazing. I've never been prouder of anyone."

For a moment, Lynx looked vulnerable. "Will you go with me? We'll have to slip away from the party long enough to hear them announce the winner, but we can go right back to the party afterward. I don't want to go alone."

Lynx didn't need to ask. "Of course. I'll cheer so loud for you that if they don't call your name, they'll wish they had."

A blush tinted Lynx's cheeks. Clint swore in that moment that he would do exactly what he said. He would look like the biggest fool in front of everyone for Lynx.

"You're the greatest man I've ever met."

Clint took the words in the chest. He wasn't, but he would be, because he could see Lynx believed. Every horrible thing he had done felt washed clean when he looked at Lynx. They would have the best life. Clint reached over and plucked a dandelion at the edge of the blanket. He brushed the soft flower down Lynx's cheek.

Lynx smiled but never slowed talking. "Did you know while everyone considers dandelions weeds, they have a ton of health benefits? They're loaded with antioxidants that help reduce inflammation, lower blood sugar, reduce cholesterol, lower blood pressure, aid in liver function, and could help you in losing weight. Of course, I don't know who's eating them to find that out. They don't look like they taste very good."

Clint rolled and tucked Lynx beneath him. "Is there anything you don't know at least a little about?"

"Football," Lynx answered with a smile. It grew. "Basketball. Golf. Basically, all sports except hockey. Oh, and fly fishing. I've never tried that, but I also don't think I would be good at it. I'm sure there are more things."

"Uh huh," Clint mumbled as he kissed Lynx's chin. He had already forgotten what they were talking about. There was a beautiful man beneath him. They were alone. It was a nice day. Clint caught himself rocking forward as his cock stirred. A small catch sounded in Lynx's breath. That was the moment Clint knew there was no going back. One way or another, he would have Lynx's cum on his skin before he was done. Making love wasn't something he normally did. Clint was more a hardcore sex kind of guy. But as Clint rolled his hips, slowly riding the friction between them, he wanted this side of them too. They were in love. He knew it in his heart. They didn't need the words or some big heart-baring confession. He felt them in every touch. Every stolen glance. This was real, and—for once—Clint was completely at peace with himself.

SIX

WHILE A LOT OF PEOPLE WERE NERVOUS TALKERS
and laughers, Lynx seemed to be the opposite. Since
their flight landed in Vegas, Lynx hadn't said a word.
It was unnerving. Clint kept eyeing him, looking for
any signs of life. Each time he looked Lynx's way,
Lynx was chewing his bottom lip and staring at
nothing. Clint made it until they were getting ready
for the release party before he broke. Lynx was fresh
from the shower, nude, and looking confused about
what he should wear. The party and awards were at
the same time and they would be hopping between
both.

From his spot on the bed, Clint watched
Lynx's anxiety visibly grow. He snagged Lynx's
waist and urged Lynx to stand between his knees

at the edge of the bed. "Talk to me, angel. What's wrong?"

Lynx blinked. His eyes seemed to focus—like he snapped back to reality. His hands smoothed across Clint's shoulders before he linked his fingers behind Clint's neck. "Sorry. I thought I had a plan in place when I packed, but now I don't know what to wear."

Without thought, Clint automatically cupped Lynx's nude ass and massaged. "You're wearing the shirt with the image of the new game on it. Promo first, remember?"

Lynx's expression turned pinched. "I still think I should wear the t-shirt that has the pride bowtie printed on it, in case I get called on stage, but I also need to promote."

Since Lynx was always kind of a wild mess, Clint didn't freak out at Lynx's oncoming panic attack. "How about this? You wear the bowtie shirt and I'll wear the game shirt. That way, between the two of us, we have everything covered."

A smile touched Lynx's lips. "You can't wear my shirt. You're too big."

Clint stood, leaving Lynx no choice but to take a step back. He peeled his shirt up and over his head before snagging the game shirt. Clint stretched the material a little before pulling it on. It molded to his body like a second skin and he would be uncomfortable as hell the entire night, but he would wear the shirt for Lynx.

Lynx's eyes danced with laughter. "You're right. That's much better promo than me wearing that shirt. Everyone will be looking at you. Goddamn." He rubbed Clint's pecs. "I should get you to model everything. Holy shit. How much time do we have?"

Clint bit back a smile. "I don't know. It depends on what you have in mind."

"Fuck." Lynx sounded adorably despondent. "There's no way we have enough time for you to dick me down the way I like."

A burst of unexpected laughter escaped Clint. He never knew what Lynx would say next. "I promise you can have me however you want after you win that award tonight."

The heat drained from Lynx's expression. The panic was back. "What if I don't win?"

Clint eyed Lynx from head to foot, letting the desire wash over him. "Then I'll have you in every way I want you and you won't even recall where you were tonight."

"Goddamn," Lynx said, sounding breathless. "I'll take that runner-up prize any night of the week." With a shake of his head, Lynx started dressing. As much as Clint hated watching Lynx cover his beautiful body, Clint still breathed an inner sigh of relief. He wished he could take Lynx's nervousness into himself and protect Lynx from the worry. Clint knew Lynx and Cage deserved to win that award. Unlike the big gaming companies, they were still hands-on. While they employed thousands for various jobs, they still did a majority of the coding and testing. Cage and Lynx always had their heads together, plotting ways to go to the next level. It was fascinating watching their pure grit transform into new creations. No one deserved recognition the way they did.

As Lynx pulled on his socks, a knock landed on the hotel room door.

Clint headed for the living room to answer.

"Shit. That would be Colt. I got lost in thought and forgot he was on his way up."

Clint froze halfway to the door at Lynx's words. His head whipped around. "I'm sorry. What did you say?"

Lynx's eyebrows rose and he nodded toward the door. "That's probably Colt. Magic and Descent is his baby. He's the creator. The brains behind the new game," he explained. "I told him we would all go down together since he's never been to one of these conventions before and doesn't know anyone. This is his big night. I'm introducing him to the world."

Clint shook his head, trying to shake off the shock of hearing Colt's name on Lynx's lips. Colt was a common name. Right? There was no way Lynx meant his ex, Colt. The chances of that had to be astronomical, right? His ex didn't create video games. Clint let it go. He was being ridiculous. Clint opened the door and his stomach dropped. The blond-haired, blue-eyed cowboy who had once been the center of Clint's every obsession stared at Clint with an equal amount of shock etching his features.

Colt broke first. "What in the hell are you doing here?"

"It's my room," Clint answered, sounding numb even to his ears.

Clint's gaze slid to the door, as if checking the number before focusing on Clint once more. "I don't understand."

Lynx appeared at Clint's side. "Come on in, Colt. I still have to get my shoes on." He turned away and headed for the loveseat, completely oblivious to the ongoing shit show. "By the way, Colt, this is Clint. Clint, this is Colt."

Colt didn't step inside the room.

Clint turned away, leaving Colt standing in the

hall. Without meeting Lynx's gaze, he headed for the bedroom, leaving the mess behind. There was no way he could go to this party now.

"What the hell? Excuse me," Lynx said over his shoulder, following Clint into the bedroom. "Just make yourself at home. I'll be back in a second." Lynx closed the bedroom door behind him and focused on Clint. "What was that?"

"I can't go."

Lynx's expression snapped closed. "Do you want to tell me why?"

Clint shook his head. "Not really, but I guess I have to. That's my ex."

Lynx's chest expanded—like he sucked in a quick breath. "The big one?"

"Yes." As Clint looked on, Lynx's face paled. Clint took it like a punch to the gut. He sat. His knees wouldn't hold him any longer. Thankfully, the bed was there to catch him.

"You were supposed to wear my shirt."

Clint's throat swelled at the pain in Lynx's voice. "I still will. Everywhere except the party. I need you to back me on this, okay? It's important for me to be better than I was with him. The old me wouldn't have cared if I ruined his big night. The new me can't do that. I have to let him have this without me there. You have no idea how much he hates me. I can't force him to have to look at me while you introduce him to the world."

"What about—" Lynx stopped mid question and visibly swallowed. For the first time since Clint sat through Lynx's phone call with his dad, Clint saw Lynx withdraw. His spark for life went into hiding. Something in his eyes dimmed. "Kiss me and I'll go."

Clint shifted to his feet and closed the distance between them. His gaze never wavered from Lynx. He needed Lynx to see his heart and understand why he had to make this choice. He had to prove he wasn't who Colt would no doubt try to convince Lynx that he was. Clint was a better man now because of Lynx. That wouldn't be true if he went to that party. Clint touched his lips to Lynx's and poured his heart into their kiss. He loved Lynx. Clint hoped Lynx could feel it.

"Go win that award," Clint whispered against Lynx's lips. "I believe in you."

Lynx took a step back. His gaze never quite met Clint's. "Sure. I'll see you later." Without a backward glance, he headed out. His voice sounded too bright and strained as he left Clint behind. "You ready, Colt? Let's go sell the hell out of your game."

Clint flinched as the hotel room door slammed

closed, taking Lynx's light away. He covered his face with both hands and sucked in a deep breath. The pains in his chest were real. It had been a long time since he felt this level of guilt and failure. The hurt in Lynx's expression was sitting on Clint's windpipe. Panic slammed into Clint. What if Lynx didn't come back? Clint would die. Lynx was his whole world. He hated himself. Clint didn't know what to do. Since Colt left him, Clint had sworn he would be different. Better. If he went to Colt's party, then he would be breaking the promise he made to himself to no longer ruin anyone else's life. But on the other side of things, he had sworn to Lynx he would be there for him. The idea of hurting Lynx was choking him, but he also needed to be able to live with himself at the end of the day. Ugh. The frustration was real. Clint didn't know if other people had to work so hard at being a good person, but Clint did. He needed help. Clint needed advice. He wanted to be with Lynx, but he also didn't want to make Colt uncomfortable.

From nowhere, a smile pulled at his lips. Only one person had offered him any decent advice as an adult. Only once did an amazing slice of wisdom save him in his time of need. WWLD... what would Lynx do? Clint knew exactly what Lynx would do in this position, and he needed to get started before he was too late. Clint wouldn't fail Lynx. He would see.

LYNX KEPT HIS GAZE LOCKED STRAIGHT AHEAD. The question he refused to ask Clint still burned in his throat. What about him? Clint had sworn he would cheer the loudest for Lynx, even if he didn't win tonight. He had looked so devastated. Lynx eyed Colt on the sly as they worked their way down the snack table, filling their plates. Colt was a million times of everything that Lynx could ever be. He was tall and muscular. Sexy. Lynx was skinny and nerdy. Colt was exotic. Without Lynx's bright and multicolored hair, he wouldn't stand out in any room. People only looked at Lynx because he was a weirdo. Everyone looked at Colt because he was Texas prime meat.

With his plate full of junk food, Lynx stood to the side at the bustling party and stared at the mound of snacks he didn't want. He had already made the release date announcement and introduced Colt. Now all he had to do was sulk. God knew he didn't need to eat anything. What if he developed a gut on top of being homely? For fuck's sake. Clint was already out of Lynx's league. Clint already didn't want to be seen with Lynx with Colt here. Lynx already didn't matter as much as preserving Colt's happiness. Goddamn. He should throw his plate away.

"Are you okay?"

Lynx pasted on a fake smile for Colt as he looked the guy's way. "Sure. Just jet-lagged, I guess. It's only a two-hour time difference, I know, but I'm still feeling it."

Colt nodded. He shifted from one foot to another. His gaze dropped to his plate. Lynx's did too. There was nothing but raw vegetables. Naturally. Lynx rolled his eyes and looked away.

"I didn't mean to cause a problem between Clint and you."

Lynx sipped his soda, minding his words. "You didn't. Austin is such a big town and a small one at the same time. It just never occurred to either of us that you two might know each other."

Colt scanned the crowd, looking everywhere but at Lynx. "So I guess you know we used to date."

Death could take Lynx any time now. His entire face hurt from faking happiness. "Yep."

Colt kept nodding—like he didn't know what to do with his head. Lynx felt a hint of guilt. This had to be uncomfortable for him too. While Lynx didn't know Colt and Clint's story, he knew it was a bad one. All of that was in the past, except it wasn't because Clint had chosen Colt's feelings over Lynx's, and it fucking stung.

Suddenly, Colt stopped nodding. His gaze fixed on Lynx and didn't budge—like his mind was finally set. "I'm about to sound like a real dick."

Lynx popped a few chips into his mouth to give himself a second. He was bad about saying every thought in his head and there were too many thoughts he needed to keep to himself in this scenario. "Okay," he said around his food.

"I don't know how much you know about Clint, or how long you've been together, but he's not a good guy."

Lynx shoved more chips in his mouth. "All right," he mumbled, almost incomprehensible around the food in his mouth.

"He..." Colt stared at Lynx while Lynx furiously chewed. To his surprise, a bright smile lit Colt's face. "You know what? Never mind. Thank you for everything you've done for me. I'm sorry Clint couldn't make it to the party with you."

Lynx swallowed. He wasn't strong enough to be quiet. "He didn't want to ruin your big night."

Colt blinked, as if Lynx shocked him. After a heartbeat, Colt shook his head. "That's not possible. No one could ruin this night for me. He shouldn't miss the whole event on my account. Everything that happened between us is all water under the bridge now. The two of you should get to enjoy this convention without a single thought for me."

"I'll be sure to let him know." Even to Lynx's ears, he sounded too bright. He wouldn't tell Clint a thing. Lynx wasn't gorgeous like Colt. He couldn't measure up, and the last thing he wanted to do was spend his night watching Clint's every move, hoping not to see him longing for Colt. It already killed Lynx that he was still Clint's second choice. He had thought he could live with that. Now he wasn't as sure any longer.

"Hey, Lynx, they're getting ready to announce the winners next door."

At the yelled words from one of his colleagues, Lynx threw his plate in the trash and headed for the door without another glance Colt's way. His stomach shook. He had thought he was prepared to lose, but he wasn't, especially now. It was one thing to watch someone else accept the award he wanted so badly with Clint at his side. It was another to lose alone, the way he always lost. Several people patted his shoulder as he passed, slipping from the party's room to the larger ballroom where the awards were being held. Lynx stayed in the back near the door so he could slip out again when he didn't win. He made it just in time.

"In the category of Game Developer of the Year, the judges have chosen..." Lynx thought he might throw up during the long pause. "Caged Lynx Games."

For a moment, Lynx didn't move. He could feel the eyes upon him, but nothing felt real. Lynx genuinely hadn't expected his company to win. His competitors were much bigger than Caged Lynx would ever be. Someone gave him a small push toward the stage and Lynx's feet finally unglued from the floor. Despite his initial shock, he still jogged up the stairs to the stage. For whatever reason, the urgent way he always moved couldn't be knocked out of him no matter what life threw his way.

Lynx shook hands with the voice actor for many games who had proclaimed him as the winner. As the gold award filled his hand, his heart shattered in his chest. No one he cared about was there. This was one of his biggest dreams come true and it was one of the emptiest moments in his life. He had no family support, Cage couldn't risk this trip to stand at his side, and Lynx knew none of that was what broke him now. Clint had chosen his ex's feelings over supporting Lynx on his big day. Lynx had never felt more alone.

He dug a small piece of paper from his pocket as he reached the podium. For several days, Lynx had scribbled a few words here and there, trying to voice what this would mean to him. But now, as Lynx stared at the crowd void of any real support, he refolded the acceptance letter he had meticulously written while dreaming Clint would be there to hear his speech. "I didn't even write a speech," Lynx said, blatantly lying to the sound of laughter. He held up the golden game controller and inspected it. "Wow. I honest to god never expected to win this."

"That's my man. I love you, baby!"

Lynx's gaze shot towards the crowd again at the yelled words. Clint stood on a chair at the back of the room, dressed in the brightest superhero costume Lynx had ever seen. His luminous smile looked even brighter with the flashing of camera lights turned his way. Lynx's throat swelled, forcing him to swallow his overwhelmed emotions. He spoke closer to the mic. "My husband Clint, everybody."

With both arms in the air, Clint cheered at the

top his lungs with the sound of laughter unable to drown him out.

Lynx unfolded the paper again. "Actually, I did write a few words," he confessed with a laugh. "What can I say? I really wanted to win." He readjusted the microphone while a round of polite chuckles filled the room. Lynx focused on Clint and spoke from the heart. "Years ago, when we were really no more than kids, Cage and I moved to Austin, Texas and risked everything on a dream. I don't think either of us considered the possibility we might fail. Even when our company made zero profit, I was at this event every year, pushing our dreams uphill with every ounce of my strength, because I had no home to crawl back to if we couldn't make this work. Plus, I knew in my heart there was no way I could love something so much and other people not see it and love it too." Lynx had to clear his throat as emotion choked him. No one truly understood how much he loved this community and what he did. It was more than a dream come true. It was a miracle he was here. "Things are very different now. Cage and I have both found our other halves. If I make a huge mistake now, and all of this is gone tomorrow, Clint will still be there. Even though I will never get to see my parents sitting in this audience, proud and accepting, I get to see Clint here and all of you. This is my real family. Thank you for letting us bring our dreams to life in the form of games, and for loving those dreams as much as we do." His gaze never wavered from Clint. "Thank you for always showing up, Clint. I love you, baby."

Lynx jogged back down the steps to the sound of applause. People stopped him, trying to congratulate him while Lynx fought to get to Clint. Thankfully, Clint found him first. The moment they stood toe to toe, Lynx couldn't see anyone else. It was like everyone disappeared or Clint eclipsed the room.

"I'm so proud of you. I knew you would win." Even though the room was loud as hell, Lynx heard Clint clear as day. The praise pierced his soul and filled a space Lynx hadn't realized was empty. He wanted to rush upstairs and celebrate alone with Clint. Lynx wanted to hear Clint confess his love again in private. Reality stole the happiness from the moment, hitting him like a ton of bricks. Colt's party still hadn't ended yet.

⸻

ADRENALINE PUMPED THROUGH CLINT'S VEINS. He had known it all the way to his soul that Lynx would win that award. Clint had never expected Lynx to admit to loving him in his speech. Of course, Clint hadn't meant to scream his love across a crowded room either. Pride in Lynx had gotten the best of him and he had gotten caught up in the moment. Clint did love Lynx, though, so it didn't really matter how or when he said it.

As he stared down at Lynx, the happiness drained from Lynx's expression. Clint's insides twisted at the sight. He needed his angel to be happy. This was his big night. Clint had dressed up for him. He was still in WWLD mode.

"What's wrong, baby?"

"The party is still going on next door."

Lynx sounded so despondent that Clint couldn't take it. Clint whipped a mask from his pocket. He had already taken that into consideration. "The costume came with a mask. I could put it on and go with you. That way, Colt doesn't have to look at me, but I can hold my sexy husband's hand." Clint took a breath. "I don't want to go back to the room alone and miss being with you, but I also don't want to be a dick, you know?"

Lynx pressed his lips together, visibly fighting a smile. "I love you."

There was no hiding Clint's happiness. "I love you too."

"I thought you were choosing his feelings over mine earlier."

Clint's smile slipped away at Lynx's confession. "Never. Maybe sometimes I don't know what the right thing to do is, because all I was taught was that real men never show emotion, but I know that I love you. I'd never purposely hurt you." Clint brushed the back of his knuckles down Lynx's cheek. He forgot they were standing in the middle of a huge crowd. Clint couldn't see anyone else. He shuffled a step closer. "Tell me how I can fix it."

"Maybe you both could come back to the party, because I don't know anyone else here, and Dex can't make it until tomorrow."

At the sound of Colt's voice, Clint turned his head. When his gaze landed on Colt, he felt nothing.

Colt flashed him a pained smile. "Sorry to interrupt. I've been standing here five minutes, waiting to talk to y'all, and I think we're blocking some people from leaving."

Clint came back to himself and glanced around. They were blocking the aisle. He automatically wrapped an arm around Lynx to keep him from getting crushed and swept him closer so people could pass. "Sorry. I forgot where we were."

Lynx pressed his face to Clint's chest—like he hid a blush. He shook with laughter. The sensation had Clint smiling. "Maybe we should head across the hall." After the aisle cleared, they moved as a group into the less crowded hallway.

Colt spoke first. "Congrats on your win, Lynx. That's amazing."

Lynx held out the award so they could inspect it. "Thank you. This is pretty cool." His gaze locked on Clint. "Where should we put it?"

"I think you may have to fight Cage for it. After all, you got to accept it. Maybe you two could share custody," Clint offered with a chuckle.

"I think we should set it on the mantel above the fireplace," Lynx said with a sniff, obviously not totally onboard with sharing.

Colt's gaze moved between them. "Wow. You two really are married. When did that happen? I didn't even know you knew each other."

Before Clint could respond, Lynx exploded into his usual hyper self. "We met several months ago through a mutual friend. Then, I decided to keep him, so I dragged him from place to place until he couldn't resist me any longer."

"Actually, I couldn't resist him from day one," Clint corrected.

Lynx ignored him and kept talking. "We got married two weeks ago when I lost a bet. See, we were already engaged. We had our marriage license and were in the middle of debating wedding venues when the topic of Dr. Who arose. I bet him that he couldn't name every person to ever play the character. He bet he could. I took his wager. We decided if I won, our honeymoon would consist of traveling across eight states to follow a convention I love to eight different venues. If he won, I had to marry him that same day. Of course, I forgot to set any rules governing how he went about naming each actor and actress. So he whipped out his phone and Googled the answer. Since I sort of hoped I would lose, and I knew he would still go with me to eight states because he loves me, I didn't argue with the blatant cheating. We got married that same day and immediately headed out to follow Zombie X Con through their west coast tour."

Clint couldn't stop smiling or staring at Lynx. He had never been happier in his life. He felt ten years younger and free. Since meeting Lynx, Clint's life had been a dream. He felt himself changing a little more every day. He had never loved anyone or anything so much.

"Wow. Sorry. I know I keep saying that, but wow. Y'all are adorable." Colt held his hand out for Clint. "It's nice to meet you, Clint. I'm pretty sure I never have before."

With a laugh, Clint shook Colt's hand. He was right. They felt like strangers now. "Congratulations on your game release. I'm sure it'll be a huge success. You have the absolute best backing you." He released Colt's hand and hauled Lynx against his side again. A familiar figure cutting through the crowd behind Colt caught Clint's attention. Dex Wise had damn near everyone's gaze moving his way. Clint didn't know if it was his dark hair and odd bluish-gray eyes or his billionaire air that held people captivated, but Clint was oddly glad to see him. He nodded the man's way. "Your husband is headed this way."

Colt lit from the inside out as he turned to greet Dex. A smile tugged at the corners of Clint's mouth. He understood that feeling of excitement at the sight of a spouse. Clint always felt that way about Lynx. His gaze moved to Lynx. Lynx chewed his bottom lip as he stared up at Clint. Clint hated the worry in his eyes. Without thought, he automatically dropped his head and captured Lynx's lips. Nothing mattered to him like Lynx's happiness. He wouldn't let Lynx question his love. In fact, now that Lynx had said the words, Clint wanted nothing more than to be alone with him. Clint's lips moved to Lynx's ear. He brushed a light kiss across its shell before speaking low and keeping their conversation private.

"Now that his husband is here, do you think anyone would notice if I stole you? You're wearing my favorite jeans with the holes in the knees. I want to peel them off."

Lynx sucked in an audible breath. "Leave everything to me." Lynx pulled away. "Hiya, Dex. It's good to see you. Look, I won an award." He flashed it Dex's way but didn't give the guy a chance to talk. "I understand you've already met my husband, Clint. He's wearing a super sexy superhero costume that I can't wait to fuck him in, so since you're here, and Colt doesn't need me, I'm going to whisk him away to make our room neighbors hate us. Let's do breakfast in the morning. My treat. I'll text you in the morning with a time."

With the hurricane known as Lynx in charge, Clint could only flash a surprised-looking Dex a quick smile before Lynx dragged him away. On the elevator, Clint ground his back teeth, praying for patience. His ability to contain his aggressive sexuality had significantly lessened since Lynx wanted him at his worst. But times like now, surrounded by people and still two floors from their room, Clint needed that control. Lynx was testing him. He stood with his back to Clint, seemingly innocent. Clint knew the truth. Lynx's hand was behind him, massaging Clint's cock through his clothes on the sly. Clint stared at the lit digital numbers on the elevator wall, slowly growing and taking them to their room. He willed the numbers to move faster. By the time the door opened, setting them free, Clint was on the edge of madness. The floor was empty when they stepped out. Lynx should have considered he would have to pay the price for teasing. The moment they were alone, Clint attacked. He easily plucked Lynx off his feet and tossed him over his shoulder. With Lynx helpless to stop him, Clint slapped his ass hard. Unfortunately, Lynx moaned and nearly crippled Clint.

"Hurry, Clint."

Clint's knees weakened at the desperation in Lynx's voice. He barely got their room door unlocked with his trembling hand. He kicked it closed behind him and ate up the floor between the door and the bedroom. When he reached the edge of the bed, Clint gently lowered Lynx, letting Lynx's body slide down his. When their gazes met, Clint's breath caught. Lynx looked turned on and in love. He was the most beautiful man in the universe to Clint.

"Let's set this over here," Clint said, taking Lynx's award and setting it on the bedside table. When he turned back Lynx's way, Lynx was already stripping. He looked half insane as his gaze landed on Clint.

"Hurry, Clint. I need you to fuck me."

A smile that felt evil even to him tugged at Clint's lips. He moved to his luggage and found the lube before tossing it on the bed. Clint took his time undressing while Lynx settled onto the bed nude and waiting. Lynx looked horny as hell. His cock stood proud. He palmed it while he watched Clint strip.

"You should use that lube, Lynx."

Lynx scrambled to grab the tube and do as ordered.

Hunger and madness clawed at Clint's insides as he watched Lynx toy with his own asshole, readying himself for Clint's dick. Even once he was nude, Clint didn't pounce. Instead, he palmed his erection and stroked. "Tell me how you want this dick."

Lynx openly writhed. "Inside me. Now."

Clint didn't budge. "You know damn well what I meant. Tell me how you want it."

Lynx rolled until he was kneeled on the edge of the bed, ass up and face buried in the mattress. "Fuck me hard, Clint. Don't hold back."

In two steps, Clint was there. He slapped Lynx's ass with both hands, palming his cheeks, and spreading them wide so he could impale Lynx's asshole with ease. Lynx didn't want him to hold back. Clint didn't. With his feet planted and while holding Lynx's hips hard enough to leave bruises, Clint slammed inside Lynx over and over. Nothing penetrated his mind beyond the pleasure. He had one goal—oblivion. His hips rolled. With his back teeth locked, Clint fucked Lynx so hard, it was like he was trying to climb inside him. He wanted to permanently make them one. The sounds Lynx made drove him. Lynx white-knuckled the covers and cried out with each thrust. Sweat rolled down Clint's back. His balls drew up tight. Lynx's muscles tensed. Clint held his breath. Lynx's asshole clamped down so hard on Clint's dick for half a second that Clint gasped. Then, Lynx's orgasm hit, and Clint saw stars as Lynx's body sucked him. Pleasure rocked him to his soul as wave after wave washed over him. Clint kept trying to get deeper, pumping Lynx's ass full of cum. He could already imagine the thick white fluid dripping back out again —like a job well done. Lynx had no idea how twisted little things like seeing Lynx leaking Clint's cum everywhere got Clint off. Those moments made him feel powerful. It was as if he owned Lynx in those moments. He had marked his territory. There was a small piece of Clint's life essence inside the man he loved. Goddamn. It was moving.

Clint eased backward, letting his dick slip from Lynx's ass before rolling Lynx onto his back. His face was red and sweaty. Lynx's eyes were unfocused. His bottom lip was swollen as if he had been biting it. In that moment, Lynx had never looked sexier. Clint crawled into bed and covered Lynx's body with his. He lightly brushed his lips across Lynx's until Lynx's lips parted, letting him in. Their tongues stroked. Clint fought for air even as he refused to give up Lynx's mouth for a proper breath. For the first time, it hit Clint. This was what love looked like. Intense and deep. Sometimes, not all that pretty, but still somehow beautiful.

"I love you." Clint whispered the words between kisses, and then deepened their kiss so Lynx couldn't respond. Each time he came up for air, Clint repeated them before stealing Lynx's ability to speak.

He didn't need to hear Lynx proclaim his love. Clint needed to be the one saying the words. His whole life, there had never been anyone who accepted him and his heart the way Lynx did. Clint needed to pour himself into Lynx right now. Maybe tomorrow night, it would be Lynx's turn to do the same. Right now, Clint needed Lynx to let him be real. Lynx always let him have his way.

LYNX CLUNG TO CLINT'S CHEST, HOLDING HIM tighter than necessary. For once, he had nothing to say. Instead, his lips kept brushing any place he could reach. If he thought too much about it, falling in love with Clint had been risky and terrifying. On paper, marrying him had been the height of lunacy. None of that had mattered at all, though. At the end of the day, Clint always showed up, even when all signs should have pointed to them being hopeless. Lynx had found his person.

"I think if I could genetically engineer the perfect person, you would be it."

Lynx's gaze shot to Clint's face at the offhand remark. "I think that might be the sweetest and geekiest thing you've ever said to me."

A sexy smile curved Clint's lips. His nose crinkled in an adorable way. "I may not be smart like you, but I can be a geek."

Lynx went up onto his elbow. "Hold up just a minute. First off, you are too smart. I could never love a stupid man. Also, I know you're brave because you wore that bright red superhero costume like a boss. But a geek? No. I don't think you have a secret geek inside waiting to jump out and argue which fictional universe is superior. You're very grounded in reality."

Clint cocked his head to one side and eyed Lynx like he considered Lynx's words. "Am I? If you'd said that to me a year ago, I would have wholeheartedly agreed. Now I wonder if I'm not a bit of a dreamer too. After all, I dared to hope you might love me, even when I was positive you couldn't possibly see anything in me." Clint toyed with Lynx's hair. "Maybe I am just dreaming."

God. Lynx hadn't known how intense love could be until he met Clint. It was almost a madness. "Maybe everyone is," Lynx said, incapable of not being a complete nerd for five seconds. "Maybe none of life is real. It's possible we're all someone else's dream." He paused when he realized how carried away he was getting. Clint wore his patient and indulgent smile. The one he always wore when Lynx followed his insane thoughts down a rabbit hole. Lynx shook his head, forcing the subject from his mind. "It doesn't matter. I love you and I don't care how that happened."

"I do," Clint said, taking Lynx by surprise. "It matters to me how you fell for me, because I don't want it to stop."

"It's too late for that." Lynx didn't care if the confession made him vulnerable. He knew Clint wouldn't take their love for granted. Clint had already learned the power of his actions, and he cared too deeply to hurt anyone else. Maybe that was Colt's loss and Lynx's gain, but Lynx had a feeling life had worked out exactly as intended. If Lynx knew nothing else, he knew they would never stop loving each other and trying to make each other better. They were what real love looked like.

SEVEN

"Are you ready for this?"

Clint nodded. "Let's do it."

"Are you sure," Lynx pressed, making Clint chuckle. Lynx obviously expected Clint to be nervous, but he was the one who looked like he was barely stopping himself from chewing his nails. "We can leave anytime you feel uncomfortable."

With a shake of his head, Clint steered Lynx toward the door. "Don't worry over me. I already woke up to my face being plastered on every activist and pride-themed news' site on the planet, as your supportive husband in the bright red superhero costume. A gay nightclub is nothing now."

Lynx didn't look any less worried. "Still, that's

online. This is in person. You're hot. People won't care you're married. They'll still flirt."

Clint stopped and focused on Lynx. "This was your idea. If you don't want to go, we won't. I'm cool to go back to the hotel room and cuddle. You're the one who said it's your duty to force me into a gay bar at least one time, as a rite of passage."

Lynx gave Clint a sharp nod, as if his mind was set. "It's better to visit your first gay bar in Vegas. That way, you won't run into anyone you know."

A snort escaped Clint. "Baby, there's no chance of me running into anyone I know no matter which state we're in."

"Not true," Lynx said, linking his arm through Clint's and heading for the door. "Just because you think everyone you know is straight, doesn't make it so. You'd be surprised how many people you meet who are sneaking away to be themselves when the sun sets. But since we're in my hometown, there's no chance you'll see anyone you know."

Clint listened to Lynx talk—the way he always did, but his gaze was locked on the first man he spotted as they crossed the threshold into the club. In a roped-off section, in the closest corner of the room, sat Raiden. He didn't look the same as he had on their date. Instead, he wore a tight black dress and heels. With his long legs crossed, Raiden sat perched on the knee of an older gentleman with salt and pepper hair. His shock froze his gaze on the man too long. Lynx busted him staring.

"Who are you looking..."

Clint glanced down at Lynx when his voice faded away. Even beneath the odd lighting inside the club, Lynx looked pale. "You've got to be fucking kidding me." Before Clint could question the outburst, Lynx was gone. He stormed across the room, heading straight for Raiden. Clint shot after him. His heart dropped into his stomach as Lynx confronted the man who had gone on a single date with Clint. In his shock and panic, it never occurred to him that Lynx shouldn't know Raiden was the man Clint had hired the one time they had fought. It wasn't until the older gentleman urged Raiden off his lap and stood to square off against Lynx that it hit Clint. It wasn't Raiden that Lynx looked ready to fight.

"Well, look at you, Papa. Where is your wife?"

Clint blinked. His gaze moved to Raiden. He looked every bit as horrified as Clint felt. Clint looked closer at the older version of Lynx. His skin tone was a bit darker and he was a hair taller than Lynx, but they had several of the same features.

"Good evening, Joseph. I see you still haven't learned to dress yourself properly. If you must know, you mother left me almost a year ago. I've been trying to call you."

Lynx practically shook with outrage. "Don't put this on me and don't call me by that name. It's only been a few months since we spoke, and I always ask about Mom. You've had plenty of chances to tell me she'd left."

"I don't know why you ask about her. She never asks about you."

Clint felt like he was the one who took the hit. Lynx looked like his father had slapped him. Without another word, Lynx turned and walked away. Clint followed. As they stepped outside, Lynx took his hand and kept going, obviously intent on never looking back.

"Are you okay?"

Lynx didn't respond.

"Joseph Hirata, I command you to stop and listen to me."

At the roared pronouncement, Lynx stopped so fast and hard that he nearly took off Clint's arm as he spun to face off against his father. "My name is Lynx Jones."

That seemed to break through the man's hard

shell a bit. He blinked. "That's ridiculous. You'll always be Joseph Hirata. That name is your birthright."

"No," Lynx said, eating up the space between them, as if he might really fight the man. "You know damn well I changed my name at eighteen, and my last name is my husband's now."

"You're married?" He sounded genuinely hurt.

Lynx wasn't letting that get to him. He looked completely done with the man he called Papa. "Yes. I'm married now and you don't get to spit on that like you have everything else. So it's Jones. In fact, you know what, I think I should be the one spitting." He took a breath, as if gearing up to say all the words.

His dad beat him to the punch. "How dare you get married without my permission. You are a disgrace to the family name."

It was the wrong thing to say. Clint took a step in the man's direction. He had listened to enough.

Lynx snapped before Clint could. "You're the disgrace." At the ice in Lynx's voice, Clint froze. He was kind of scared to move. "In fact, I'm embarrassed when anyone asks me about you. I'm ashamed to admit you're my father." The elder Hirata paled as Lynx handed him back the words the man had fed Lynx his entire life. "It's humiliating to admit that you are a complete failure at being a father. That you blew any chance at having a future with your son. I don't want anyone to know about the years of browbeating and mental abuse, because it's truly demeaning to admit how long I tolerated your presence in my life." He held his hand out and Clint automatically moved to take it. Their fingers linked, but Lynx's gaze never wavered from his father. "I'm officially rescinding your invitation to be part of my life. I have a new family now. Go back inside and find someone you can pay to call you Papa. You've lost the right to ever hear the name from me again, Touma Hirata."

Lynx turned away with Clint at his side. Every day Lynx found a way to make Clint proud. He knew Lynx's father's words hurt, but he also knew Lynx would never show it. Clint would never stop being all the family Lynx would ever need. As long as Clint lived, Lynx would know his worth.

INSIDE, LYNX SEETHED. HE WANTED TO PRETEND his father's words didn't hurt. They always would. That dig about his mom never asking about him cut to the bone. The only thing saving him was having

Clint at his side. His gaze slid Clint's way. He was so strong and sexy. A smile tugged at Lynx's lips. Fuck that guy who had raised him. In truth, Lynx had raised himself. There had never been a parent that hugged him or sang about their love. He had Clint for that now. None of those years of neglect mattered any longer.

Lynx leaned closer into Clint's side. He wrapped both arms around Clint's massive arm and hugged. Clint kissed his forehead and untangled himself from Lynx's hold so he could wrap Lynx in his embrace. As they reached their rental car, Clint twisted and walked Lynx backward until he had him pinned against the car.

"Are you okay, sexy angel?"

The concern in Clint's eyes warmed Lynx's heart. All the resentment and anger of seeing his father melted away as Lynx snaked his arms around Clint's neck and lured him even closer. "I'm perfect. I have you."

"Do you want to talk about what just happened?"

Lynx shook his head. A smile snapped to his lips. A chuckle escaped him. "How was your first trip to a gay club?"

Clint's sexy smile made the ridiculous question

worthwhile. "It was memorable. Let's never do it again."

"Awww," Lynx cooed. "I didn't mean to ruin the experience for you."

"It's not you. You make everything amazing." Clint dipped his head and nuzzled Lynx's neck. "I just don't think clubbing is for me." His lips skimmed Lynx's throat. He somehow managed to shuffle even closer. His hard body had Lynx on the verge of panting. "I'd rather be in bed with you, if I'm being honest," Clint said against Lynx's skin. "As much as I appreciate your every attempt to introduce me to new things, this is all I need." Clint's hands skimmed down Lynx's body until he cupped Lynx's ass.

Lynx clung to Clint's shoulders. "We should go back to the room."

"Mhmm," Clint hummed as he licked Lynx's throat. "Give me a minute. This spot tastes too good to give up yet."

Lynx's eyes fell closed. They had all night. In fact, they had the rest of their lives. Clint could take all the time he needed. Lynx would cling to him and soak up the love. Maybe Lynx didn't have great parents, but he had an awesome family. Clint was his tribe now. Choosing Clint was the single greatest risk Lynx had ever taken. He was everything good and real. Lynx was so goddamn thankful for this life. He would never take it for granted.

---

*... **READ ON FOR A DELETED SCENE.***

Something nagged at the back of Clint's mind as he packed, readying to go back home. They had one more night in Vegas, and then they'd get to be still for a little while. He was ready, but there was something here that just wasn't setting right with him. His gaze slid Lynx's way. He looked at peace as he worked on packing his suitcase. Clint still couldn't shake this feeling in his gut.

"Call your mom."

Lynx's gaze shot his way. A surprised sounding chuckle escaped him. "No. You heard my dad. He said my mom never even asks about me. I'm not about to get kicked by the same horse twice while we're here."

Clint snorted. "Did you just make a cowboy joke? I can't believe it. Lynx Jones made a cowboy joke. Still, I'm not letting this go. You should call your mom."

Lynx went back to packing. "Nope."

With a sigh, Clint closed the distance between

them. He felt of Lynx's pockets until he found his phone. Clint dug it out and handed it to Lynx. "Call her."

Lynx didn't reach for the phone. He shook his head. "I can't do it."

With a small growl, Clint held the phone up to Lynx's face, unlocking it. He scrolled through Lynx's contacts until he found Lynx's mom. He pressed the call button and put the phone on speaker, ignoring Lynx's evil glare that promised retribution. If Lynx's mother was like his father, Clint was ready to permanently boot her from Lynx's life. But Lynx had once said his mom wasn't that bad, and he had a feeling about this one.

A female voice filled the air. "Lynx?" She sounded almost panicked.

Lynx blinked, as if shocked by her tone. "Hey, Mom."

"Oh my god, Lynx. I'm so happy to hear your voice." She sniffed—like she was crying. "I was afraid to call."

A line appeared between Lynx's brows. He took the phone from Clint. "Why? You know you can call me anytime. Every time I talk to Papa, he says you're out of town. Of course, now I know that's not true."

"No, baby. I haven't been on a trip in ages. Your

dad said you didn't want to talk to me. That I was the reason you moved away, and you didn't want anything else to do with me."

Lynx dropped to sit on the edge of the bed—like his knees gave out. "I didn't know. I miss you."

Clint had to look away. He had known this was eating at Lynx, but he hadn't known how to help. He had already lost Lynx once to interfering. Now, he was glad he hadn't let this go.

"I miss you too, baby. Tell me everything. I want to hear about everything I've missed."

A choked-sounding laugh burst from Lynx, making Clint smile. "That's a lot. I'm married now."

Silence met his bombshell.

Clint stared at Lynx while Lynx stared at the phone with his bottom lip between his teeth.

Finally, Lynx broke. "Are you still there?"

"Yeah." Her voice sounded muffled—almost like she had her mouth covered. She sniffed again and cleared her throat. "Did you finally break Cage down?"

Lynx smiled. "No. He's married now too, but not to me. To the perfect guy for him. My husband's name is Clint. Actually, he's here too. He's the one who forced me to call." Lynx's gaze lifted to Clint's. "Say hi, Clint."

"Hello. It's nice to meet you, ma'am."

"Ma'am," she repeated with a chuckle. "It's nice to meet you too, Clint. Thank you for making Lynx call and welcome to the family... such as it is."

"We're in town for the convention," Lynx said fast, as if worried—once again—she would reject him.

"Really? That's great. I didn't know there was a convention in town, but I would love to see you."

Lynx blinked rapidly, as if her words nearly brought him to tears. "Is it okay if Clint and I take you to dinner?"

"I would love that. We have a lot of catching up to do." She sounded like she meant it. Clint drew a steady breath. No one understood how certain he always was that he was fucking up everything he touched. It was nice to make a good decision for once.

Lynx smiled and met Clint's gaze. "Agreed. We'll pick you up around seven. Is that okay?"

"Sounds great. I'll be ready, and Lynx, I love you, sweetie."

"I love you too, Mom."

"See you at seven."

"Yeah. See you then."

Lynx disconnected the call and set the phone aside. For a moment, he stared at nothing before focusing on Clint. Clint's heart skipped a beat at the emotion in Lynx's expression. "You really just did that."

Clint blinked. He wasn't sure of Lynx's tone. He shifted from one foot to the other. "Yeah, well, I love you."

Lynx shook his head and snorted. "Did you even have a plan?"

"Not really. I just thought your father is a bastard who obviously just says whatever he thinks will hurt you the most, even when there's no chance of any of it being true. I mean, who could be ashamed of you? So, I figured, if he lies about all that to hurt you, then he was probably lying about your mom too."

Lynx was back to silently staring at Clint, making him want to shift nervously again. "I love you. You know that, right?" Before Clint could answer, Lynx stood and closed the distance between them. He held Clint's waist and shuffled close. Clint was captivated by the love pouring from his eyes. Lynx didn't seem to need a response. "You're the most amazing man on the planet and I wonder if you even realize it."

That was bullshit, but Clint didn't call him on it. After all, he liked that Lynx thought that he was great, even though it wasn't true. "I love you. I need you to be happy."

Something dark passed over Lynx's features. "What about you? Are you happy?"

Clint's eyebrows snapped together. "Of course. Why wouldn't I be? I have you."

Lynx loosened Clint's belt. He lifted one shoulder in a half shrug. His voice turned sultry. "I just thought, maybe you could be happier."

Clint didn't think that was possible, but he was willing to let Lynx try.

IF YOU'D LIKE TO READ RAIDEN'S STORY, HIS BOOK is the second book in my Messy Hearts series, *Soul-Wrecked*.

PLEASE CONSIDER LEAVING A REVIEW AT THE retailer where this book was purchased. Reviews really help with a book's visibility, which ensures I can continue writing. Thank you, Charity.

ABOUT THE AUTHOR

Charity Parkerson is an award winning and multi-published author with several companies. Born with no filter from her brain to her mouth, she decided to take this odd quirk and insert it in her characters.

*Eight-time Readers' Favorite Award Winner
   *2015 Passionate Plume Award Finalist
   *2013 Reviewers' Choice Award Winner
   *2012 ARRA Finalist for Favorite Paranormal Romance
   *Five-time winner of The Mistress of the Darkpath

Connect with her online:

--Join   my   street   team:
facebook.com/TeamCharityParkerson
   --Website: charityparkerson.com
   --Facebook:
facebook.com/authorCharityParkerson

facebook.com/TheMenofSin
--Twitter: twitter.com/CharityParkerso